John Phin

An Exact Reprint of the Famous Century of Inventions of the

Marquis of Worcester

John Phin

An Exact Reprint of the Famous Century of Inventions of the Marquis of Worcester

ISBN/EAN: 9783743389748

Manufactured in Europe, USA, Canada, Australia, Japa

Cover: Foto ©Raphael Reischuk / pixelio.de

Manufactured and distributed by brebook publishing software
(www.brebook.com)

John Phin

An Exact Reprint of the Famous Century of Inventions of the

Marquis of Worcester

EDWARD SOMERSET, SECOND MARQUIS OF WORCESTER.

OF THE FAMOUS

Century of Inventions.

OF

THE MARQUIS OF WORCESTER.

(First Published in 1663.)

WITH

INTRODUCTION, NOTES AND A LIFE OF THE AUTHOR,

BY

JOHN PHIN.

WITH PORTRAIT AFTER A PAINTING BY VANDYKE.

———◆———

NEW YORK:
THE INDUSTRIAL PUBLICATION COMPANY.
1887.

PREFACE.

Our object in reprinting the famous "CENTURY OF INVENTIONS," as it is generally called, is not to give any novel solutions of the problems which it sets forth, but simply to place this famous and exceedingly interesting production within the reach of ordinary book-buyers. Although it has been several times reprinted, it is so scarce that copies are to be had only with considerable difficulty. Of the first edition, published in 1663, very few copies are to be found outside the shelves of a few well-known public libraries. It is said that this is largely due to the fact that all the copies that were procurable were bought up and burned by a rival inventor (Savary), who claimed to be the first inventor of the steam engine, Of subsequent reprints it will be found on inquiry that they have been so much sought after and read that they have been literally "thumbed out of existence," as the genial author of "The Book Hunter" expresses it in regard to similarly popular books.

Under these circumstances it is to be hoped that our present offering will prove acceptable to a large number of those who are interested in the history of inventions and of mechanics.

J. P.

Cedar Brae,
October, 1887.

LIFE

OF

EDWARD SOMERSET,

SECOND MARQUIS OF WORCESTER.

———◆———

Edward Somerset alias Plantagenet,[*] Second Marquis of Worcester, like many of the wisest and best of this earth — nay, like the wisest and best—bore on his escutcheon the Baston Sinister. He was descended from John of Gaunt, Duke of Lancaster, son of Edward the Third. Charles, the natural son of Henry Beaufort, third Duke of Somerset, in that line, assumed the surname of Somerset, and from him was descended the famous author of "The Century of Inventions," who was the eldest son of Henry Lord Herbert and Anne, sole daughter and heir of John Lord Russell, eldest son of Francis Russell, Earl of Bedford. He was born

———————————

[*] See Patent granted by Charles the First on the 1st of April, 1644: "Charles, by the Grace of God, King of England, Scotland, France and Ireland, defender of the faith, etc., to our right trusty and right well beloved cousin, Edward Somerset alias Plantagenet, Lord Herbert, Baron Beaufort, of Caldicate, Grismond, Chepstow, Ragland and Gower, Earl of Glamorgan, son and heir apparent of our entirely beloved cousin, Henry, Earl and Marquis of Worcester, greeting." Etc., etc., etc.

early in 1601 the exact date being unknown. During his
father's life-time he was known first as Lord Herbert, and
afterwards as Earl of Glamorgan. On the death of his
father he succeeded to the titles of Earl and Marquis of
Worcester.

His education appears to have been conducted privately
under the tutorship of a Mr. Adams. It does not appear
that he was entered at any of the great English colleges,
though it is possible that he may have been connected with
some foreign university. Be this as it may, it is quite certain that his education was as complete and thorough as
that of any young man of his time.

In the year 1628 he married Elizabeth, daughter of Sir
William Dormer. She bore him one son and two daughters.
The son, Henry Somerset, was created first Duke of Beau-
fort.

It is supposed that shortly after his marriage he retired to
Raglan Castle and devoted himself to study and experiment,
but of this we have no record.

In the year 1635 (May 31st) he lost his wife, to whom he
was greatly attached. Four years later he married Mar-
garet, second daughter of Henry O'Brien, Earl of Thomond.
He obtained by his second wife some valuable possessions,
and he also became connected with some of the most
wealthy and powerful families in Ireland. By his second
wife he had one daughter who died while quite young.

It is an unfortunate circumstance that we know very little
of the daily life of the Marquis at this period, and nothing at

all of his pursuits, studies and inventions, except in a most general way. Even the exact dates of important events in his life are unknown, and the length of time during which he was imprisoned in the Tower is a matter of conjecture. That he continued his scientific and mechanical pursuits even during the early tumults of the civil war is pretty certain, and that some of his inventions were put in operation, at Raglan Castle, on a scale of considerable magnitude, seems more than probable from the following anecdote related by Dr. Bayly: "At the beginning of this Parliament (Nov. 1640) there were certain rustics who came into Raglan Castle to search for arms, his lordship* being a Papist. The Marquis met them at the castle gate, desiring to know whether they came to take away his money, seeing they intended to disarm him. They stated that they made the application merely in consequence of his being a recusant. To which he replied, 'He was a peer of the realm, and no convict recusant, therefore the law could not in reason take notice of any such things.' Finding some sharp and dubious expressions coming from the Marquis, they were at last willing to take his word; but he, not willing to part with them on such easy terms, had before resolved to return them one fright for another. With that view he conveyed them up and down the castle, until at length he brought them over a high bridge that arched over the moat that was between the castle and the great tower, wherein the Lord Herbert had newly con-

---

* The father of the famous Marquis.

trived certain water-works, which, when the several engines and wheels were to be set a-going, much quantity of water, through the hollow conveyances of the aqueducts, was to be let down from the top of the high tower; which, upon the first entrance of these wonderful asinegoes, the Marquis had given order that these cataracts should begin to fall, which made such a fearful and hideous noise, by reason of the hollowness of the tower, and neighboring echoes of the castle, and the waters that were between, and round about, that there was such a roaring as if the mouth of hell had been wide open, and all the devils conjured up, occasioning the poor silly men to stand so amazed as if they had been half dead; and yet they saw nothing. At last, as the plot was laid, up came a man staring and running, crying out '*Look to yourselves my masters, for the lions are got loose.*' Whereupon the searchers tumbled so over one another escaping down the stairs, that it was thought one half of them would break their necks, never looking behind them until out of sight of the castle."

Troublous times were now approaching. Charles the First was in sore need of money, and Lord Herbert and his father advanced him large loans from their personal estate. In addition to this they raised and sustained a considerable body of troops. Up to this time the highest dignity attained by the family was that of Earl of Worcester. On the 2nd of November, 1642, Henry, (the father of the famous Edward) was created Marquis of Worcester. The civil war now raged, and Raglan Castle was garrisoned by troops maintained by the Somersets in the interest of the King. The scientific and mechanical skill of Lord Herbert, (the future Marquis) were here brought into play, and a powder mill was erected on the estate and actively operated for the supply of ammunition to the royal troops.

As a military man, however, Lord Herbert does not seem to have achieved much success. His troops were defeated by the Parliamentary forces, and his pecuniary losses were so enormous that he was made a poor man for the rest of his life.

In 1645 he was sent to Ireland by the King with a commission to raise a body of 10,000 Irish troops for service in England to oppose the parliamentary forces. To secure the aid of the Catholics in this effort, Lord Herbert, recently created Earl of Glamorgan, was empowered to offer the Romish dignitaries the most liberal terms, not only as regarded toleration, but in the matter of lands, titles, etc., to be placed in their possession. This arrangement was, however, completely upset by certain wholly unlooked for events. The Popish Archbishop of Tuam, President of Connaught, and one of the Supreme Council at Kilkenny, going into Ulster to visit his diocese, and put into execution an order for arrears of his Bishopric, granted to him by that Council, met with a body of Irish troops marching to besiege Sligo, and joined with them. When they came near that town, the garrison made a sally on the 17th of October, charged the troops, and utterly routed them, killing the Archbishop in the encounter. Amongst the baggage of the Archbishop was found an authentic copy, attested and signed by several bishops, of the treaty concluded with them by the Earl of Glamorgan.   The result of this disclosure was that Lord Digby charged the Earl with suspicion of high treason, and moved that his person be secured.   The charge being fully substantiated, the Earl was committed to the custody of the Constable of Dublin Castle in the condition of a close prisoner.   After a brief confinement he was liberated on bail, but under the condition that he should not leave the Kingdom of Ireland.

Meanwhile Raglan Castle, the family seat and the scene of his early studies and experiments, was taken by General Fairfax after a prolonged seige.   The letters and papers were carried off and the castle ordered to be demolished. It is probable that in the dispersion and destruction of these papers we have lost the records of many of the early experiments and inventions made by the Marquis.

These accumulated misfortunes no doubt hastened the death of his father, which occurred in December, 1646.

Very soon after these events matters were so arranged that he was enabled to go to France, where he remained in exile for four or five years.   That some arrangement look-ing to his voluntary exile was made with the government is more than probable, as the Marquis was too honorable to leave in the lurch his friends, the Marquis of Clanricarde and the Earl of Kildare, who were on his bond for ten thousand pounds each.

On the 30th of January, 1649, Charles the First was executed; the commonwealth was established on the 6th of February following, and the Protectorate under Cromwell in 1654. Meanwhile Charles the Second had escaped to the continent and set up a migratory court. Although the Marquis was not a constant attendant at this court, he appears to have been in communication with them, and in 1652 he was sent to England for private intelligence as well as for supplies. Unfortunately, however, he was recognized, made prisoner, and committed to the tower, where he remained for a period variously estimated at from two to six years. During his confinement he wrote the famous book known as "A Century of Inventions," which, however, was not published until 1663, though it was supposed that several manuscript copies were made and circulated amongst his friends. One of these is now in the British Museum, and is interesting on account of certain slight variations from the printed book.

In 1660 Charles the Second returned to England and was placed upon the throne of his fathers. One would suppose that a man who had suffered so much in attestation of his loyalty would have been most liberally treated, but we find that, although the estates of the Marquis were restored, they were heavily encumbered and greatly despoiled. The timber had been removed, the buildings were in ruins, and the sources of income were but trifling. He therefore took up his residence in London, where, in the hopes of retrieving his fortune, he devoted himself to the prosecution of his studies and the perfecting of his inventions, though it would seem without any very marked financial success.

Four years after the publication of the "Century"—on the 3rd of April, 1667—he died in London, and on the 19th of the same month he was buried in the family vault within the Parish Church of Raglan.

Such is a meagre outline of the life of the Marquis of Worcester. Those who desire to follow out the details of his political relations more closely will find much material in the Life by Henry Dircks—a crude and ill-digested performance, which should be called a collection of materials for a biography, rather than a biography.

That the Marquis of Worcester was a keen student and an enthusiastic inventor, there can be no doubt. That the results which he attained have been greatly over-estimated is very certain, but the wonder is that he should have accomplished anything at all when we consider the troublous times in which his lot was cast.

As a man he was loyal, brave and honest, qualities not always found in high places in those days. Unfortunately, for himself, he was, during a great part of his life, attached to the losing side, and when the tide of success turned he was too old to secure the favor of such a frivolous and sensual monarch as Charles the Second.

INTRODUCTION.

If we except those who have taken an active controversial part in religion or politics there is no man in regard to whom such positively opposite opinions have been entertained, as the Marquis of Worcester. Dircks, in the Dedication prefixed to his Life of the Marquis, affirms that it would be "impossible to name his compeer either amongst the highest nobility or the most eminent scientific celebrities of Europe, during the last two centuries." In other words, Newton, Davy, Faraday, Watt, Stephenson, and all the other stars in the bright galaxy which stretches across the last two two hundred years, pale before the effulgence of the fame of the Marquis of Worcester!! On the other hand Walpole speaks of the "Century of Inventions" as "an amazing piece of folly," and rates the author as little better than a madman! It is pretty certain that the truth lies between these two extremes, for the one is the conclusion of a man of trinkets and trifles who never in his life grappled with a serious subject and conquered it, and the other is the outcome of mere toadyism on the part of a man who evidently wished to ingratiate himself with certain aristocratic families.

Unfortunately, for the Marquis, the labors of Mr. Dircks

have rendered certain the fact that to him we owe absolutely nothing so far as inventive progress is concerned. He may have constructed steam engines more perfect than those turned out by the best factories of the present day; he may have perfected inventions, which, if now understood, would render both telegraph and telephone useless, and his "Water-Commanding Engine" may have been not only "Semi-omnipotent" but actually *omnipotent*, and yet it is no injustice to him and no ingratitude on our part for us to say that we owe him NOTHING, for with all the efforts of Mr. Dircks and all the facilities placed at his command, as regards old papers, records, models, etc., there has not been brought to light one scrap of writing, or one fragment of a model, that tends to show that the Marquis ever developed a successful invention or that he ever carried one to such a degree of completion as would enable a modern mechanic to profit to any extent by his labors.

It is therefore very obvious that we owe none of our mechanical or inventive progress to him. Whether he actually succeeded in perfecting the inventions that he describes, and especially, whether or not he was the real inventor of the steam engine, are questions which will be attacked by those who desire to gratify their antiquarian curiosity, but not by those who desire to render to the name of a benefactor the homage which gratitude prompts.

Many of the inventions described by the Marquis are frivolous and useless. He gives no clue to his ciphers, but it is the simplest of all tasks to devise methods which will conform to all the conditions stated in his book; the only difficulty is that in these days the deciphering of cryptographs has made such progress that any such ciphers would be useless. A mere tyro in the art would be able to decipher them and in a few minutes force them to give up their true meaning.

That many of the alleged inventions described in the Century were solved only in the imagination of the Marquis can hardly be doubted by any intelligent student. For example, No. 56 is a very perfect description of a common form of so-called perpetual motion—that is to say, it is one of those forms which are almost certain to occur to every active mechanical mind that attempts to solve this famous problem. We have known it to be invented a dozen times by persons whose efforts and ideas were entirely independent of each other, and who had never heard of the thing before. We have had models of this contrivance brought to us, and so strong was the hold that the theoretical idea had taken upon the minds of the inventors that although in every case the models failed to operate yet this was invariably attributed to the mechanical defects and rude workmanship of the model and not to any fallacy lurking in the theory. And every editor of a popular scientific journal and every person having much to do with inventors, will no doubt testify to the same experience.

It is a fact well known to all who are actually brought into contact with mechanical progress that the inventive world is full of embryo inventions whose maturity is an impossibility. At one time our, Patent Office required models of all inventions capable of being so illustrated. As a general rule the office accepted what were called "dummy" models—that is to say, models that merely showed the form and arrangement of the parts without actually working. In particular cases the office had the power to demand "working" models, but these were not often required. Now every patent agent will testify that the percentage of inventions which seemed feasible in drawings and dummy models and yet failed in actual practice was very large. And, so plausible did these schemes seem that the authors would have had no hesitation in risking their lives on the results; far less would they have hesitated to describe them as "inventions which they had tried and perfected." So that we are far from impugning the veracity of the Marquis when we say that many of these things existed only in his imagination, for it must be borne in mind that every inventor is gifted with a vivid imagination; indeed, if defective in this respect, he never could be an inventor.

Those who will carefully study the inventions described in the "Century" will be surprised to see how many of them have been brought to a degree of perfection of which the Marquis could have had no idea. Not only has the power of steam been so developed that the claims of the Marquis have been far exceeded, but our telegraphs, telephones, armored ships, land turrets and other contrivances throw far in the shade anything ever conceived or named by him. But, when we read his wonderful descriptions we cannot but accord to him a power of vision far in advance of his day. He had a marvellous insight into the future, and unbounded faith in the possibilities of science and mechanics, and the probability is that if he had closely settled down to the hard work of thorough investigation, and the prosaic study of facts and principles, he would have been the real inventor of the modern steam engine. But not only did he fall upon evil times, his mind was too enthusiastic and flighty for such work, and he spread over a "Century" of inventions that power which he ought to have confined to one or two.

Amongst the questions which always occur when the name of the Marquis of Worcester is brought forward, are those relating to the invention of the steam engine. Prof. Robison and some others broadly claim that he was the inventor of this modern aid to civilization, while Arago claims the like for De Caus, others claim it for Savery, and the friends of other inventors make like claims. The thoughtful student will see that none of these claims are well founded. The development of the Steam Engine was a gradual process, proceeding in some cases along distinct and unconnected lines, which in every case served to develop some useful principle, but which did not always produce a practical result, capable of utilization in the modern machine.

The principal stages of this course of invention seem to have been the following:

1. The discovery of the expansive force of steam.

2. Its direct application to the production of mechanical motion.

3. Its direct application to the raising of water in closed vessels.

4. Its use in the formation of a vacuum so as to produce mechanical motion.

5. Its application to the direct movement of a piston in both directions.

At every one of these stages various minor improvements were made, any one of which would, if not superseded by better, have made the fame and fortune of any inventor, but to no one inventor do we owe our advancement through more than one stage. Let us briefly glance at these several stages.

The expansive power of steam was no doubt discovered at a very early period in the history of man's progress. Indeed, it is quite certain that it antedates many of our well-defined historic periods, such as the bronze and iron ages. It was probably discovered as soon as men had constructed rude vessels of earthen ware in which they could cook their food. The lids of these vessels would often be raised by steam; explosions of pent-up vapor would occur, and even in the infancy of the arts, men would be taught to respect the tremendous power which now does us such noble service.

We can easily imagine the consternation of the ancients at some of these tremendous manifestations, and we can easily suppose that they would be attributed to the working of some Genie or Spirit, for all the invisible forces were so regarded by men in early times. Our modern word *gas* is nothing but the word *ghost* in a different form, and it came to be applied to invisible airs, because these were supposed to be subterranean spirits. So the name of the metal *Cobalt* is merely a transformation of the word *Kobold*, the name of an evil spirit who was supposed to haunt mines, and change good metal to worthless alloy. In the hands of the ancient priests, steam played an important part in many Pagan ceremonies, and therefore we may safely conclude that this stage of the discovery of steam as a source of power antedates all history.

The same is true of the second stage. In his work entitled " Spiritalia," Hero, of Alexandria, describes three modes in which steam might be employed as a mechanical power : 1, to raise water by its elasticity ; 2, to elevate a weight by its expansive force, and 3, to produce a rotary motion by its reaction in escaping from the side of a tube. The latter works on the same principle that operates the well-known Barker's water-mill. Hero does not claim these inventions as his own, but, as has been well said, " though posterity is really not indebted to him for the invention, it is still more beholden to him for the bequest of his description, than if he had been the inventor and had omitted to describe it." The invention of Branca, and also the well known modification of Branca's device, in which a jet of steam is made to act directly on the buckets or vanes of a breast-wheel, come under this head.

In the third stage we find steam used in close vessels and pressing directly upon the water to be raised. This was a direct step in advance, though in some of its forms it was no doubt invented at a very early period. The crudest form of the device is that of which the so-called engine of De Caus is an illustration. In this " engine " the entire body of water to be raised must first be heated above the boiling point—an arrangement which is utterly impracticable so far as any useful *mechanical* purpose is concerned. This device is, however, very old—much older than De Caus.

It would of course soon be found that it was not necessary to heat the water to be raised; that steam from a separate boiler would be much more economical. This method was fully described by Porta in 1601, and is still in use in a simple and tolerably efficient form of water-raising engine.

The fact that when steam is condensed by cold, a vacuum is formed, was well known in very ancient times. The old steam blowers or Eolipiles were frequently filled by utilizing this principle, and it was not a great step from the mere raising of water into an Eolipile to the raising of a weight by the use of a piston. Pistons for raising water antedate any recorded form of the steam engine, and their adaptation to the production of mechanical movements by the pressure of the atmosphere, did not require any great stretch of the inventive faculty.

The fifth stage in which steam was caused to act directly on a piston, was the culmination of the invention of the steam engine. An infinite number of modifications, and of additional devices and improvements may have been added, but this was the fundamental idea the adoption of which brought success.

To which of these stages the inventions of the Marquis belonged we have no means of knowing. There is not a scrap of drawing, a fragment of a model, or an intelligible description remaining to aid us on this point. True, we have many sketches, and so-called restorations, but they are all the products of the fancy and the inventive powers of biographers and commentators.

As regards the engine at Vauxhall, it may, for aught we know, have been a mere pump. Two very intelligent travellers visited the works at times considerably apart, and both speak of the use of horses for driving the engines. A steam engine, worked by horses, is certainly a curious invention.

Historians have indulged in much speculation as to the causes which delayed the invention of the steam engine to so late a period. It is acknowledged on all hands that the properties and powers of steam were tolerably well understood, and all the mechanical elements of a successful engine had been invented—the crank, the piston, etc. And the mechanical skill of the ancients has furnished a subject for many a lecturer on the " lost arts." Why then was not the steam engine produced? Simply because it was not needed. What would have been the use of a motive power to a people who had no machinery for it to drive? The Greeks and Romans had not even a threshing machine, far less spinning machinery, power looms, or rolling mills. All their mechanical work was done by hand-power, and so long as the spinning wheel was turned by women and the shuttle driven by men, of what use could a steam engine have been to them?

In the history of the arts, and sciences we find that the progress of each depends greatly upon that of the others. Astronomy and physiology came to a standstill until the science and practice of optics were so improved as to place the telescope, the spectroscope and the microscope at their command. Since then the progress made in these departments has been simply marvellous. In the arts we find that every new demand gives rise to new inventions and new discoveries. As soon as the English mines required power of some kind to keep them free from water, pumps suited to the purpose were invented. At first these pumps were worked by hand, but as soon as greater power became necessary new inventions were made and horse-power was applied. This enabled the mines to be carried to a greater depth, and then a still more powerful motor was needed, and as soon as this became apparent the steam engine was invented.

In the arts as in daily life, the extent of our wants is the measure of our civilization.

NOTE.

In the following pages we give a verbatim reprint of the Edition of 1663—the only one known to have been published during the life of the Marquis.

There is in the British Museum (Harleian MS. No. 2428) a manuscript copy of the Century. Partington affirms that this copy is in the handwriting of the Marquis, but such is not the case. It is evidently a mere copy made by some one for his own convenience before the work was printed. The top of the title page of the MS. copy bears the words "from August ye 29th to Sept. ye 21st, 1659" This is supposed to indicate the time occupied in copying it.

The MS. copy differs in several places from the printed edition. These variations we have given in foot notes, so that the reader may have the exact text of both the printed and the written copy.

In the MS. copy, however, No. 88 instead of being a description of a Brazen Head, is a description of "A Stamping Engine" for coining money. The description is as follows:—" An engine without ye least noyse, knock or use of fyre, to coyne and stamp 100 lb. in an houre by one man."

A
CENTURY
OF THE
Names and Scantlings
OF SUCH
INVENTIONS,

As at prefent I can call to mind to
have tried and perfected, which
(my former Notes being loft) I
have, at the inftance of a powerful Friend, endeavoured now in
the Year 1655, to fet thefe
down in fuch a way as may fuffi-
ciently inftruct me to put any of
them in practice.

―――― *Artis & Naturæ proles.*

LONDON:
Printed by *J. Grifmond* in the year 1663.

TO THE

KINGS

Most Excellent MAJESTY.

Sir,

Scire meum nihil est, nisi me scire hoc sciat alter, *saith the poet, and I most justly in order to Your Majesty, whose satisfaction is my happiness, and whom to serve is my onely aime, placing therein my* Summum bonum *in this world: Be therefore pleased to cast Your gracious Eye over this Summary Collection, and then to pick and choose. I confess, I made it but for the superficial satisfaction of a friends curiosity, according as it is set downe ; and if it might now serve to give aime to Your Majesty how to make use of my poor Endeavours, it would crowne my thoughts, who am neither covetous nor ambitious, but of deserving Your Majesties favour upon my own cost and charges ; yet, according to the old English Proverb,* It is a poor Dog not worth whistleing after. *Let but Your Majesty approve, and I will effectually perform to the height of my Undertaking : Vouchsafe but to command, and with my Life and Fortune I shall chearfully obey, and* maugre *envy, ignorance and malice, ever appear*

Your Majesty's
Passionately-devoted, or
otherwise dis-interested
Subject and Servant,
WORCESTER.

To the Right Honourable

And to the KNIGHTS, CITIZENS, AND BURGESSES *of the Honourable House of Commons ;* NOW *assembled in Parliament.*

My Lords and Gentlemen,

Be not startled if I address to all, and every of you, this Century of Summary Heads of wonderful things, even after the Dedication of them to His most Excellent Majesty, since it is with His most gracious and particular consent, as well as indeed no wayes derogating from my duty to His Sacred Self, but rather in further order unto it, since your Lordships, who are his great Council, and you, Gentlemen, His whole Kingdom's Representatives (most worthily welcome unto Him,) may fitly receive into your wise and serious considerations what doth or may publickly concern both His Majesty and His tenderly-beloved People.

Pardon me if I say (my Lords and Gentlemen) that it is joyntly your parts to digest to His hand these ensuing particulars, fitting them to His palate, and ordering how to reduce them into practice in a way useful and beneficial both to His Majesty and His Kingdom.

Neither do I esteem it less proper for me to present them to you, in order to His Majesty's service than it is to give

into the hands of a faithful and provident Steward whatsoever dainties and provisions are intended for the Master's
diet; the knowing and faithful Steward being best able to
make use thereof to his Master's contentment and greatest
profit, keeping for the morrow what ever should be over-
plus or needless for the present day, or at least, to save
something else in lieu thereof. In a word (my Lords and
Gentlemen), I humbly conceive this *Simile* not improper,
since you are His Majesty's provident Stewards, into whose
hands I commit my self with all properties fit to obey you,
that is to say, with a heart harbouring no ambition, but an
endless aim to serve my King and Countrey: and if my endeavors prove effectual (as I am confident they will), his
Majesty shall not onely become rich, but his people likewise,
as Treasurers unto Him; and His Pierless Majesty, our
King, shall become both belov'd at home and fear'd abroad,
deeming the riches of a king to consist in the plenty enjoyed
by His People.

And the way to render Him to be feared abroad is, to
content his People at home, who then, with heart and
hand, are ready to assist him; and whatsoever God blesseth
me with to contribute towards the increase of His Revenues
in any considerable way, I desire it may be employed to the
use of His People; that is, for the taking off such Taxes or
Burthens from them as they chiefly groane under, and by a
Temporary necessity onely imposed upon them, which being
thus supplied will certainly best content the King and satisfie
His People, which I dare say is the continual Tend of all

your indefatigable pains, and the perfect demonstrations of your Zele to His Majesty, and an evidence that the Kingdoms Trust is justly and deservedly reposed in you. And if ever Parliament acquitted themselves thereof, it is this of yours, composed of most deserving and qualified Persons—qualified, I say, with your affection to your Prince, and with a tenderness to His People; with a bountiful heart towards Him, yet a frugality in their behalfs.

Go on, therefore, chearfully (my Lords and Gentlemen), and not onely our gracious King, but the King of Kings will reward you, the Prayers of the People will attend you, and His Majesty will, with thankful arms, embrace you. And be pleased to make use of me and my endeavors to enrich them, not my self; such being my onely request unto you, spare me not in what your Wisdoms shall find me useful, who do esteem myself not onely by the Act of the Water-commanding Engine (which so chearfully you have past), sufficiently rewarded, but likewise with courage enabled to do ten times more for the future; and my Debts being paid, and a competency to live according to my Birth and Quality setled, the rest shall I dedicate to the service of our King and Countrey by your disposals: and esteem me not the more or rather any more, by what is past, but what 's to come; professing really, from my heart, that my Intentions are to outgo the six or seven hundred thousand pounds already sacrificed, if countenanced and encouraged by you, ingenuously confessing that the melancholy which hath lately seized me, (the cause whereof none of you but may easily guess,) hath, I dare say, retarded more advantages to the public service than modesty will permit me to utter: And now revived by your promising favors, I shall infallibly be enabled thereunto in the Experiments extant, and comprised under these heads practicable with my directions by the unparall'd workman, both for trust and skill, *Casper Kaltoff's* hand, who has been these five-and-thirty years as in a school, under me imployed, and still at my disposal, in a place by my great expences made fit for publick service, yet lately like to be taken from me, and consequently from the service of King and Kingdom, without the least regard of above ten thousand pounds expended by me, and through my Zele to the Common good; my Zele, I say, a field large enough for you (my Lords and Gentlemen) to work upon.

The Treasures buried under these heads, both for War, Peace, and Pleasure, being inexhaustible; I beseech you pardon me if I say so; it seems a Vanity, but comprehends a Truth; since no good Spring but becomes the more plentiful by how much more it is drawn, and the Spinner to weave his webb is never stinted but further inforc'd.

The more then that you shall be pleased to make use of my Inventions, the more Inventive shall you ever find me; one Invention begetting still another, and more and more improving my ability to serve my King and you; and as to my heartiness therein, there needs no addition, nor to my readiness a spur. And therefore (my Lords and Gentlemen) be pleased to begin, and desisist not from commanding me till I flag in my obedience and endeavors to serve my King and Country.

For certainly you'l find me breathless first t'expire,
Before my hands grow weary, or my legs do tire.

Yet, abstracting from any Interest of my own, but as a Fellow-Subject and Compatriot, will I ever labor in the Vineyard, most heartily and readily obeying the least summons from you, by putting faithfully in execution what your Judgments shall think fit to pitch upon amongst this Century of Experiences, perhaps dearly purchased by me, but now frankly and *gratis* offered to you. Since my heart (methinks) cannot be satisfied in serving my King and Country, if it should cost them anything; As I confess, when I had the honor to be neare so obliging a Master as His late Majesty, of happy memory, who never refused me his Ear to any reasonable motion: And as for unreasonable ones, or such as were not fitting for him to grant, I would rather to have dyed a thousand deaths than ever to have made any one unto him.

Yet whatever I was so happy as to obtain for any deserving Person, my Pains, Breath and Interest employed therein, satisfied me not, unless I likewise satisfied the Fees; but that was in my Golden Age.

And even now, though my ability and means are shortened, the world knows why my heart remains still the same; and be you pleased, my Lords and Gentlemen, to rest most assured, that the very complacency that I shall take in the executing your ·Commands shall be unto me a sufficient and an abundantly-satisfactory reward.

Vouchsafe therefore to dispose freely of me, and whatever lieth in my power to perform; first, in order to His Majesty's service; secondly, for the good and advantage of the Kingdom; thirdly, to all your satisfactions, for particular profit and pleasure to your individual selves, professing that in all and each of the three respects, I will ever demean my self as it best becomes,

My Lords and Gentlemen,

Your most passionately-bent Fellow-Subject in
His Majesty's service, Compatriot for the
publick good and advantage, and a most
humble servant to all and every of you.

WORCESTER.

A CENTURY

OF THE

Names and Scantlings of

Inventions by me already practised.

---

1. Several sorts of Seals, some shewing by scrues, others by gages fastening or unfastening all the marks at once; others by additional points and imaginary places, proportionable to ordinary Escocheons[1] and Seals at Arms, each way palpably and punctually setting down (yet private from all others but the Owner and by his assent) the day of the Moneth, the day of the Week, the Moneth of the Year, the Year of our Lord, the names of the Witnesses, and the individual place where any thing was sealed, though in ten thousand several places, together with the very number of lines contained in a Contract, whereby falsification may be discovered and manifestly proved, being upon good grounds suspected.

Upon any of these Seals a man may keep Accompts of

---

[1] Escucheons.

Receipts and disbursements, from one Farthing to an hundred millions, punctually shewing each pound, shilling, peny, or farthing.

By these seals, likewise, any Letter, though written but in English, may be read and understood in eight several languages, and in English itself to clean contrary and different sense, unknown to any but the Correspondent, and not to be read or[1] understood by him neither, if opened before it arrive unto him; so that neither Threats nor hopes of Reward can make him reveal the secret, the Letter having been intercepted and first opened by the Enemy.

2. How ten thousand Persons may use these seals to all and every of the purposes aforesaid, and keep their secrets[2] from any but whom they please.

3. A Cypher and Character so contrived, that one line, without returns and[3] circumflexes, stands for each and every of the 24. Letters; and as ready to be made for the one letter as the other.

4. This invention refined, and so abbreviated that a point onely sheweth distinctly and significantly any of the 24. letters; and these very points to be made with two pens, so that no time will be lost, but as one finger riseth the other may make the following letter, never clogging the memory with several figures for words and com-

---

1 nor to be.

2 secrets private.

3 or—*for* and.

bination of letters, which with ease, and void of confusion, are thus speedily and punctually, letter for letter, set down by naked and not multiplied points. And nothing can be less than a point, the Mathematical definition of[2] being, *Cujus pars nulla.* And of a motion no swifter imaginable then[3] *Semiquavers* or *Releshes*, yet applicable to this manner of writing.

5. A way, by a Circular motion, either along a Rule or Ring-wise, to vary any Alphabet, even this of Points, so that the self-same Point, individually placed, without the least additional mark or variation of place, shall stand for all the 24. letters, and not for the same letter twice in ten sheets writing; yet as easily and certainly read and known as if it stood but for one and the self-same letter constantly signified.

6. How at a Window, far as Eye can discover[4] black from white, a man may hold discourse with his Correspondent without noise made or notice taken; being, according to occasion given and means afforded, *Ex re nata,* and no need of Provision beforehand; though much better if foreseen, and means prepared for it, and a premeditated course taken by mutual consent of parties.

7. A way to do it by night as well as by day, though as dark as Pitch is black.

---

[1] combinations.

[2] of it.

[3] than what expresseth even.

[4] discern.

8. A way how to level and shoot Cannon by night as well as by day, and as directly; without a platform or measures taken by day, yet by a plain and infallible rule.

9. An Engine, portable in one's Pocket, which may be carried and fastened on the inside[1] of the greatest Ship, *Tanquam aliud agens*, and at any appointed minute, though a week after, either of day or night, it shall irrecoverably sink that Ship.

10. A way from a mile off to dive and fasten a like Engine to any Ship, so as it may punctually work the same effect either for time or execution.

11. How to prevent and safeguard any Ship from such an attempt by day or night.

12. A way to make a Ship not possible to be sunk, though shot an hundred times betwixt wind and water by Cannon, and should lose a whole Plank, yet in half an hours time, should be made as fit to sail as before.

13. How to make such false Decks, as in a moment should kill and take prisoners as many as should board the Ship, without blowing the Decks up or destroying them, from being reducible, and in a quarrer of an hours time should recover their former shape, and to be made fit for any imployment without discovering the secret.

14. How to bring a force to weigh up an Anchor, or to do any forcible exploit, in the narrowest or[2] lowest room in

---

[1] the side.

[2] and—*for* or.

any Ship, where few hands shall do the work of many; and many hands applicable to the same force, some standing, others sitting, and[1] by virtue of their several helps, a great force augmented in little room, as effectual as if there were sufficient space to go about with an Axle-tree, and work far from the Centre.

15. A way[2] how to make a Boat work it self against Wind and Tide, yea both without the help of man or beast; yet[3] so that the Wind or Tide, though directly opposite, shall force the Ship or Boat against itself; and in no point of the Compass, but it shall be as effectual as if the wind were in the Pupp, or the stream actually with the course it is to steer, according to which the Oars shall row, and necessary motions work and move towards the desired Port or point of the Compass.

16. How to make a Sea-castle or Fortification Cannon proof, and capable of a thousand men, yet sailable at pleasure to defend a passage; or, in and hour's time, to divide itself into three Ships, as fit and trimmed to sail as before: And even whilest it is a Fort or Castle, they shall be unanimously steered, and effectually be driven by an indifferent strong wind.

17. How to make upon the *Thames* a floting Garden of

---

1 and yet.

2 a way—*omitted.*

3 but—*for* yet.

pleasure, with Trees, Flowers, Banquetting-Houses, and Fountains, Stews for all kinds of fishes, a reserve for Snow to keep Wine in, delicate Bathing places, and the like; with musick made with[1] Mills, and all in the middest of the stream where it is most rapid.

18. An Artificial Fountain, to be turned like an Hourglass, by a child in the twinkling of an eye; it[2] holding a great quantity of water, and of force sufficient to make snow, ice, and thunder, with a[3] chirping and singing of birds, and shewing of several shapes and effects usual to Fountains of pleasure.

16. A little engine within a Coach, whereby a child may stop it, and secure all persons within it, and the Coachman himself, though the horses be never so unruly[4] in a full career; a child being sufficiently capable to loosen them in what posture soever they should have put themselves, turning never so short, for a child can do it in the twinkling of an eye.

20. How to bring up water Balance-wise, so that as little weight or force as will turn a Balance will be onely needful, more then the weight of the water within the Buckets, which counterpoised,[5] empty themselves one into

---

[1] by—*for* with.

[2] yet—*for* it.

[3] the—*for* a.

[4] and running.

[5] counterpoise, and empty.

the other, the uppermost yielding its water, (how great a quantity soever it holds), at the self-same time the lower-most taketh it in, though it be an hundred fathom high.

21. How to raise water constantly with two Buckets onely day and night, without any other force then its own motion, using not so much as any force, wheel or sucker, nor more pulleys than one on which the cord or chain rolleth, with a bucket fastened at each end. This I confess[1] I have seen and learned[2] of the great Mathematician Claudius[3] his studies at *Rome*, he having made a Present thereof unto a Cardinal; and I desire not to own any other mens[4] inventions, but if I set down any, to nominate likewise the inventor.

22. To make a River in a Garden to ebbe and flow constantly, though twenty foot over, with a childs force, in some private room or place out of sight and a competent distance from it.

23. To set a Clock in[5] a Castle, the water filling the[6] Trenches about it[7]; it shall shew by ebbing and flowing, the Hours, Minutes, and Seconds and all the comprehensible

---

[1] confess to have.

[2] in the great Mathematician's study, Claulus at Rome.

[3] Claulus.

[4] man's.

[5] as within a.

[6] and the.

[7] about it shall show the hours, minutes, and seconds by ebbing.

motions of the Heavens and Counterlibation[1] of the Earth
according to *Copernicus.*

24. How to increase the strength of a Spring to such a
height as to shoot Bumbasses and Bullets of an hundred
pound weight a Steeple height, and a quarter of a mile off
and more, Stone-bow-wise; admirable for Fire-works, and
astonishing of besieged Cities, when, without warning given
by noise, they find themselves so forcibly and dangerously
surprised.

25. How to make a Weight that cannot take up an hundred pound and yet shall take up two hundred pound,
and[2] at the self-same distance from the Centre; and so, pro-
portionally, to millions of pounds.

26. To raise weight as[3] well and as forcibly with the drawing back of the Lever, as with the thrusting it[4] forwards; and
by that means to lose no time in motion or strength. This I
saw in the *Arcenal* at *Venice.*[5]

27. A way to remove to and fro huge weights with
a most inconsiderable strength from place to place.
For example, Ten Tunne with ten pounds, and less; the

---

[1] counterlibration.

[2] and—*omitted.*

[3] so—*for* as.

[4] of it.

[5] at Venice in the Arsenal.

the said ten pounds not to fall lower than it makes the ten Tunne to advance or retreat upon a Level.

28. A Bridge, portable in[1] a Cart with six horses, which in a few hours time may be placed over a river half a mile broad, whereon with much expedition, may[2] be transported Horse, Foot and Cannon.

29. A portable Fortification able to contain five hundred fighting men, and yet[3] in six hours time, may[4] be set up and made Cannon-proof, upon the side of a River or Pass, with Cannon mounted upon it, and as complete as a regular Fortification, with Half-moons and Counterscarps.

30. A way in one nights time to raise a Bulwork twenty or thirty foot high, Cannon-proof, and Cannon mounted upon it, with men to over-look, command and batter a Towne; for though it contain but four Pieces, they shall be able to discharge two hundred Bullets each hour.

31. A way how safely and speedily to make an approach to a Castle or Town-wall, and over the very Ditch at Noonday.

32. How to compose an universal Character methodical and easie to be written, yet intelligible in any Language; so that if an English-man write it in English, a French-man,[5] Ita-

---

1 upon.

2 there may be.

yet *omitted.*

4 able to be.

5. man *omitted.*

lian, Spaniard, Irish,[1] Welsh, being Scholars; yea Grecian or Hebritian, shall as perfectly undertand it in their owne Tongue as if they were perfect English, distinguishing the Verbs from the Nouns, the Numbers, Tenses, and Cases, as properly expressed in their own Language as it was written in English.

33. To write with a Needle and Thred, white, or any color upon white or[2] any other[3] color, so that one stitch shall significantly shew any letter, and as readily and as easily shew the one letter as the other, and fit for any Language.

34. To write by a knotted Silk string, so that every knot shall signifie any letter with Comma, Full point, or Interrogation, and as legible as with Pen and Ink upon white paper.

35. The like, by the fringe of Gloves.

36. By stringing of Bracelets.

37. By Pinck'd Gloves.

38. By holes in the bottom of a Sieve.

39. By a Lattin, or Plate Lanthorn.[4]

40. By the Smell.

41. By the Taste.

42. By the Touch.

---

[1] Irish and.

[2] or upon.

[3] other *omitted*.

[4] plate candlestick Lanthorn.

By these three Senses as perfectly distinctly and uncon-fusedly, yea as readily as by the sight.

43. How to vary each of these, so that ten thousand may know them, and yet[1] keep the understanding part from any but their Correspondent.

44. To make a Key of a Chamber door, which to your sight hath its Wards and Rose-pipe but Paper-thick, and yet at pleasure in a minute of an hour, shall become a perfect Pistol, capable to shoot through a Brest-plate commonly of Carabine-proof, with Prime, Powder and Firelock, undis-coverable in a strangers hand.

45. How to light a Fire and a Candle at what hour of the night one awaketh, without rising or putting ones hand out of the bed. And the same thing becomes[2] a serviceable Pistol at pleasure; yet by a stranger, not knowing the secret, seemeth but a dexterous Tinder-box.

46. How to make an artificial Bird to fly which way and as long as one pleaseth, by or against the wind, sometimes chirping, other times hovering, still tending the way it is de-signed for.

47. To make a Ball of any metal, which thrown into a Pool or Pail of water shall presently rise from the bottom, and constantly shew by the *superficies* of the water the hour of the day or night, never rising more out of the water then just to the minute it sheweth of each quarter of the hour;

---

1 yet *omitted*.

2 becomes to be.

and if by force kept under water, yet the time is not lost, but recovered as soon as it is permitted to rise to the *superficies* of the water.

48. A scrued Ascent, instead of Stairs, with fit landing places to the best Chambers of each Story, with Back-stairs within the Noell of it, convenient for servants to pass up and down to the inward Rooms of them, unseen and private.

49. A portable Engine, in way of a Tobacco-tongs, whereby a man may get over a wall, or get up again being come down, finding the coast proving[1] unsecure unto him.

50. A complete light portable Ladder, which taken out of ones Pocket, may be by himself fastened an hundred foot high to get up by from the ground.

51. A Rule of Gradation, which with ease and method reduceth all things to a private correspondence, most useful for secret Intelligence.

51. How to signifie words and a perfect Discourse, by[2] jangling of[3] Bells of any Parish-Church, or by any Musical Instrument within hearing, in a seeming way of tuning it; or of an unskilful beginner.

53. A way how to make hollow and cover a Water-scrue, as big and long as one pleaseth, in an easie and cheap way.

54. How to make a Water-scrue tite, and yet transparent, and free from breaking; but so clear, that one may palpably

---

see the water or any heavy thing how and why it is mounted by turning.

55. A double Water-scrue, the innermost to mount the water, and the outermost for it to descend more in number of threds, and consequently in quantity of water, though much shorter than the innermost scrue, by which the water ascendeth, a most extraordinary help for the turning of the scrue to make the water rise.

56. To provide and make that all the Weights of the descending side of a Wheel shall be perpetually further from the Centre then those of the mounting side, and yet equal in number and heft to[1] the one side as the other. A most incredible thing, if not seen, but tried before the late King (of blessed memory)[2] in the *Tower*, by my directions, two Extraordinary Embassadors accompanying His Majesty, and the Duke of *Richmond* and Duke *Hamilton*, with[3] most[4] of the Court attending Him. The Wheel was 14. foot over, and 40. Weights of 50. pounds apiece. Sir *William Balfore*,[5] then Lieutenant of the *Tower*,[6] can justifie it, with several others. They all saw, that no sooner these great

---

1 of *for* to.

2 of happy and glorious.

3 and—*for* with.

4 most part.

5 Belford.

6 and yet liveing, can.

Weights passed the Diameter-line of the lower[1] side, but they hung a foot further from the Centre, nor no sooner passed the Diameter-line of the upper[2] side, but they hung a foot nearer. Be pleased to judge the consequence.

57. An ebbing and flowing Water-work in two Vessels, into either of which the water standing at a level, if a Globe be cast in, instead of rising it presently ebbeth, and so remaineth untill a like Globe be cast into the other Vessel, which the water is no sooner sensible of, but that[3] Vessel presently ebbeth, and the other floweth, and so continueth ebbing and flowing untill one or both of[4] the Globes be taken out, working some little effect besides its own motion, without the help of any man within sight or hearing: But if either of the Globes be taken out, with ever so swift or easie a motion, at the very instant the ebbing and flowing ceaseth; for if during the[5] ebbing you take out the Globe, the water of that Vessel presently returneth to flow, and never ebbeth after, untill[6] the Globe be returned into it, and then the motion beginneth as before.

58. How to make a Pistol to discharge a dozen times with

---

[1] upper.

[2] lower.

[3] the

[4] of—*omitted.*

[5] that—*for* the.

[6] unless—*for* untill.

one loading, and without so much as once new priming requisite, or to change it out of one hand into the other, or stop ones horse.

59. Another way as fast and[1] effectual, but more proper for Carabines.

60. A way with a Flask appropriated unto it, which will furnish either Pistol or Carabine with a dozen Charges in three minutes time, to do the whole execution of a dozen[2] shots, as soon as one pleaseth, proportionably.

61. A third way, and[3] particular for Musquets, without taking them from their Rests to charge or prime, to a like execution, and as fast as the Flask, the Musquet containing but one Charge at a time.

62. A way for a Harquebuss, a Crock, or Ship-musquet, six upon a carriage, shooting with such expedition, as[4] without danger one may charge, level, and discharge[5] them sixty times in a minute of an hour, two or three together.

63. A sixth way,[6] most excellent for Sakers, differing from the other, yet as swift.

64. A seventh, tried and approved before the late King

---

1 and as

2 of 12.

3 and—*omitted.*

4 as that.

5 level and discharge—*omitted.*

6 way—*omitted.*

(of ever blessed memory) and an hundred Lords and Commons, in a Cannon of 8. inches half quarter, to shoot bullets
of 64. pounds weight, and 24. pounds of pouder, twenty
times in six minutes; so clear from danger, that after all were
discharged, a Pound of Butter did not melt, being laid upon
the Cannon-britch, nor the green Oile discoloured that was
first anointed[1] and used between the Barrel thereof, and the
Engine, having never in it nor within six foot but one
charge at a time.

65. A way that one man in the Cabin may govern
the[2] whole side of Ship-musquets, to the number (if need require) of 2. or 3000. shots.

66. A way that against[3] several Advenues to a Fort or
Castle, one man may charge fifty Cannons playing, and
stopping when he pleaseth, though out of sight of the Cannon.

67. A rare way, likewise, for musquetoons fastened to the
Pummel of the Saddle, so that a Common Trooper cannot
misse to charge them with twenty or thirty bullets at a time,
even in full career.

*When first I gave my thoughts to make Guns shoot often, I
thought there had been but one only exquisite way inventible,
yet by several trials and much charge, I have perfectly tried all
these.*

---

[1] It and.

[2] a—*for* the.

[3] against the.

68. An admirable and most forcible way to drive up water by[1] fire, not by drawing or sucking it upwards, for that must be as the philosopher calleth it, *Intra[2] sphæram activitatis*, which is but at such a distance. But this way hath no Bounder, if the Vessels be strong enough; for I have taken a piece of a whole Cannon, whereof the end was burst, and filled it three quarters full of water,[3] stopping and scruing up the[4] broken end; as also the Touch-hole; and making a constant fire under it, within 24. hours it burst and made a great crack: So that having a way[5] to make my Vessels, so that they are strengthened by the force within them, and the one to fill after the other. I have seen the water run[6] like a constant Fountaine-stream, 40. foot high; one Vessel of water rarified by fire, driveth up 40.[7] of cold water. And a man that tends the work is but to turn two Cocks, that one Vessel of water being consumed, another begins to force and[8] refill with cold water, and so successively, the fire being tended and kept constant, which the self-same Person may likewise

---

[1] with—*for* by.

[2] *infra.*

[3] of water omitted.

[4] that—*for* the.

[5] found a way.

[6] to run.

[7] driving 40. of.

[8] and that to re-fill.

abundantly perform in the interim between the necessity of[1] turning the said Cocks.

69. A way how a little triangle[2] scrued Key, not weighing a Shilling[3], shall be capable and strong enough to bolt and unbolt, round about a great Chest, an hundred Bolts through fifty Staples, two in each, with a direct contrary motion, and as many more from both sides and ends; and at the self-same time shall fasten it to a place, beyond a mans natural strength to take it away: and in one and the same turn both locketh and openeth it.

70. A Key with a Rose-turning pipe, and two Roses pierced through endwise the Bit thereof,[4] with several handsomly-contriv'd Wards, which may likewise do the same effects[5].

71. A key perfectly square, with a Scrue turning within it and more conceited then any of the rest,[6] and no heavier than the triangle-scrued Key, and doth the same effects.

72. An Escocheon[7] to be placed before any of these Locks, with these properties:

---

1 necessity of *omitted.*

2 triangle and.

3 not weighing a shilling *omitted.*

4 together—*for* thereof.

5 effect.

6 other—*for* rest.

7 Schuchlon.

1. The owner (though a woman) may with her delicate hand, vary the wayes of coming to open the Lock ten millions of times, beyond the knowledge of the Smith that made it, or of me who invented it.

2. If a stranger open it, it setteth an Alarm a-going, which the stranger cannot stop from running out; and besides, though none should be within hearing, yet it catcheth his hand as a Trap doth a Fox; and though far from maiming him, yet it leaveth such a mark behind it, as will discover him if suspected; the Escocheon[1] or[2] Lock plainly shewing what monies he hath taken out of the Box to a farthing, and how many times opened since the owner hath been in it.[3]

73. A transmittible Gallery over any Ditch or Breach in a Town-wall, with a Blinde and Parapit Cannon-proof.

74. A Door, whereof the turning of a Key, with the help and motion of the handle, makes the hinges to be of either side, and to open either inward or outward, as one is to enter or to[4] go out, or to open in half.

75. How a Tape or Ribbon-weaver may set down a whole discourse, without knowing a letter, or interweaving any thing suspicious of other secret than a new-fashioned Ribbon.

---

[1] Scuchlon.

[2] or the.

[3] at it.

[4] to omitted.

76. How to write in the dark as streight as by day or candle-light.

77. How to make a man to fly; which I have tried with a little Boy of ten years old in a Barn, from one end to the other, on a Hay-mow.

78. A Watch to go constantly, and yet needs no other winding from the first setting on the Cord or Chain, unless it be broken, requiring no other care from one then to be now and then consulted with concerning the hour of the day or night; and if it be laid by a week together, it will not erre much, but the oftener looked upon the more exact it sheweth the time of the day or night.

76. A way to to lock all the Boxes of a Cabinet, (though never so many) at one time, which were by particular Keys[1] appropriated to each Lock, opened severally and independent the[1] one of the other, as much as concerneth the opening of them, and by these[2] means cannot be left opened unawares.

80. How to make a Pistol Barrel no thicker then a Shilling, and yet able to endure a Musquet proof of Powder and Bullet.

81. A Combe-conveyance carrying of[3] Letters without suspicion, the head being opened with a Needle-scrue draw-

---

1 the *omitted.*

2 this—*for* these.

3 of *omitted.*

ing a Spring towards them[1], the Comb being made but after an usual form carried in ones Pocket.

82. A Knife Spoon, or Fork in an usual portable Case, may have the like conveyances in their handles.

83. A Rasping-mill, for Harts-horn, whereby a child may do the work of half a dozen men, commonly taken up with that work.

84. An Instrument whereby persons[2] ignorant in Arithmetic may perfectly observe Numerations[3] and Substractions[3] of all Summes and Fractions.

85. A little Ball made in the shape of a Plum or Pear, being[4] dexterously conveyed or forced into a bodies mouth, shall presently shoot forth such and so many Bolts of each side and at both ends, as[5] without the owners Key, can neither be opened or[6] filed off, being made of tempered Steel, and as effectually locked as an Iron Chest.

86. A chair, made *a-la-mode*, and yet a stranger being perswaded to set in't, shall have immediately his armes and thighs lock'd up beyond his own power to loosen them.

87. A Brass mould to cast Candles, in which a man may

---

1 one—*for* them,

2 a person,

3 numeration and subtraction.

4 which being.

5 as that.

6 nor.

make 500. dozen in a day, and adde an ingredient to the tallow which will make it cheaper, and yet so that the Candles shall look whiter and last longer.

88. [1] How to make a Brazen or Stone head, in the midst of a great Field or Garden, so artificial and natural, that though a man speak never so softly, and even whispers into the ear thereof, it will presently open its mouth, and re-solve the Question in French, Latine, Welsh, Irish or English, in good terms uttering it out of his mouth, and then shut it untill the next Question be asked.

89. White Silk, knotted in the fingers[2] of a Pair of white Gloves, and so contrived without suspicion, that playing at *primero*, at cards, one may without clogging his memory keep reckoning of all Sixes, Sevens and Aces, which he hath discarded.[3]

90. A most dexterous Dicing Box, with holes transparent, after the usual fashion, with a Device so dexterous, that with a knock of it against the Table the four good Dice are fastened, and it[4] looseneth four false Dice made fit for his purpose.

91. An artificial Horse, with Saddle and Caparizons fit

---

[1] An engine without ye least noyse, knock, or use of fyre, to coyne and stamp 100. lb. in an houre by one man.

[2] finger.

[3] without foul play.

[4] It *omitted.*

for running at[1] the ring, on which a man being mounted, with his Lance in his hand, he can at pleasure make him start, and swiftly to run his career, using the decent posture[2] with *bon grace*, may take the Ring as handsomly and running as swiftly as if he rode upon a Barbe.

92. A scrue, made like a Water-scrue, but the bottom made of Iron-plate Spade wise, which at the side of a Boat, emptieth the mud of a Pond, or raiseth Gravel.

93. An Engine whereby one man may take out of the water a Ship of 500. Tun, so that it may be calked, trimmed and repaired, without need of the usual way of stocks, and as easily let it down again.

94. A little Engine portable in ones Pocket, which placed to any door, without any noise, but one crack, openeth any door or gate.

95. A double Cross-bow, neate, handsome, and strong, to shoot two Arrows, either together, or one after the other, so immediately, that a Deer cannot run two steps, but, if he miss[3] of one Arrow, he may be reach'd with the other, whether the Deer run forward, sideward, or start backward.

96. A way to make a Sea-bank so firm and Geometrically-strong, that a stream can have no power over it; excellent, likewise, to save the Pillar of a Bridge, being far cheaper and stronger then Stone-walls.

---

[1] at *omitted.*

[2] postures.

[3] be missed.

97. An Instrument whereby an ignorant person may take any thing in Perspective, as justly, and more than the skilfullest Painter can do by his eye.

98. An Engine, so contrived, that working the *Primum mobile* forward or backward, upward or downward,[1] circularly or corner-wise, to and fro, streight, upright or downright, yet the pretended Operation continueth, and advanceth none of the motions above-mentioned, hindering, much less stopping, the other; but unanimously, and with harmony agreeing they all augment and contribute strength unto the intended work and operation : and, therefore, I call this *a Semi-omnipotent Engine,* and do intend that a Model thereof be buried with me.

99. How to make one pound weight to raise an hundred as high as one pound falleth, and yet the hundred pound descending doth[2] what nothing less than one hundred pound can effect.

100. Upon so potent a help as these two last-mentioned Inventions a Water-work is, by many years experience[3] and labour, so advantageously by me[4] contrived, that a Child's force bringeth up an hundred foot high an incredible quan-

---

[1] forwards or backwards, upwards or downwards.

[2] to do.

[3] expences—*for* experience.

[4] by me—*omitted.*

tity of water, even two foot Diameter, so naturally, that the work will not be heard even into the next Room; and with so great ease and Geometrical Symmetry, that though it work day and night from one end of the year to the other, it will not require forty shillings reparation to the whole Engine, nor hinder ones day-work[1]. And I may boldly call it *The most stupendious work in the whole world:* not onely with little charge, to drein all sorts of Mines, and furnish Cities with water, though never so high seated, as well to keep them sweet, running through several streets, and so performing the work of Scavengers, as well as furnishing the inhabitants with sufficient water for their private occasions; but likewise supplying rivers with sufficient to maintaine and make them portable[2] from Towne to Towne, and for the bettering of Lands all the way it runs; with many more advantageous, and yet greater effects of Profit, Admiration, and Consequence. So that deservedly I deem this Invention to crown my Labors, to reward my Expences, and make my Thoughts acquiesce in way of further Inventions: This making up the whole Century, and preventing any further trouble to the Reader for the present, meaning to leave to Posterity a Book, wherein under each of these Heads the means to put in execution and visible trial all and every of these Inventions, with the shape

---

[1] The sentence beginning "so naturally" and ending "ones daywork," is not found in the MS. copy.

[2] make navigable—*for* make them portable.

and form of all things belonging to them, shall be Printed by Brass-plates.

In Bonum Publicum,

et

Ad Majorem DEI *Gloriam.*[1]

The following passage, added as a postscript to the MS., does not appear in the edition of 1663:

[1] " Besydes many omitted, and some of three sorts willingly not set downe, as not fitt to be divulged, least ill use may bee made thereof; butt to shew that such things are also within my knowledge, I will here in myne own cypher set down one of each, not to be concealed when duty and affection obligeth me."

THE CONTENTS.[1]

	No.
Seals abundantly significant, - - - - -	1
Private and particular to each owner, - - -	2
An one-line cypher, - - - - - - -	3
Reduced to a point, - - - - - -	4
Varied significantly to all the 24. letters, - - -	5
A minute and perfect discourse by colors,[2] - - -	6
To hold the same by night,[3] - - - - - -	7
To level cannons by night, - - - - -	8
A ship-destroying engine, - - - - - -	9
How to be fastened from aloof, and under water, -	10
How to prevent both, - - - - - - -	11
An unsinkable ship, - - - - - - -	12
False destroying decks, - - - - - -	13
Multiplied[4] strength in little room, . - - - -	14
A boat driven against wind and tide, - - - -	15

1 " Index."

2 " A *mute* yet perfect discourse, as far distant as eye can reach by day to discern colors."

3 " Though never soe darke."

4 " Multiplying."

	No.
A sea-sailing fort,	16
A pleasant floating garden,	17
An hour-glass fountain,	18
A coach-saving engine,	19
A balance water-work,	20
A bucket-fountain,	21
An ebbing and flowing river,	22
An ebbing and flowing castle clock,[1]	23
A strength-increasing spring,	24
A double drawing engine for weights,[2]	25
A to and fro lever,	26
A most easy level draught,	27
A portable bridge,	28
A moveable fortification,	29
A rising bulwark,	30
An approaching blind,	31
An universal character,	32
A needle alphabet,	33
A knotted string alphabet,	34
A fringe alphabet,	35
A bracelet alphabet,	36
A pinked glove alphabet,	37
A sieve alphabet,	38
A lanthorn alphabet,	39

---

1 " Flowing clock."

2 *For weights*—wanting in the MS.

No.

An alphabet by the { smell, - - - - - 40
taste, - - - - - - 41
touch, - - - - - 42

A variation of all and each of these,[1] - - - - 43

A key pistol, - - - - - - - 44

A most conceited tinder-box, - - - - - 45

An artificial bird, - - - - - - - 46

An hour water-ball, - - - - - - 47

A screwed ascent of stairs, - - - - - 48

A tobacco-tongs engine, - - - - - 49

A pocket-ladder, - - - - - - 50

A rule of gradation, - - - - - - 51

A mystical jangling of bells, - - - - - 52

An hollowing of a water-screw, - - - - 53

A transparent water-screw, - - - - - 54

A double water-screw, - - - - - 55

An advantageous change of centres, - - - 56

A constant water-flowing and ebbing motion, - · - 57

An often-discharging pistol, - - - - - 58

An especial way for carabines, - - - - 59

A flask charger, - - - - - - - 60

A way for musquets, - - - - - - 61

A way for a harquebuss, or crock, - · - - 62

For sakers[2] and minyons, - - - - - 63

---

[1] *and each of these*—wanting.

[2] Forsacres.

	No.
For the biggest cannon,[1]	64
For a whole side of[2] ship musquets,	65
For guarding several avenues to a town,	66
For musquetoons on horseback,	67
A fire water-work,	68
A triangle key,	69
A rose key,	70
A square key, with a turning screw,	71
An escutcheon for all locks,	72
A transmittable gallery,	73
A conceited door,	74
A discourse woven in tape or ribbon,[3]	75
To write in the dark,	76
A flying man,	77
A continually going watch,[4]	78
A total[5] locking of cabinet boxes,	79
Light pistol barrels,	80
A combe-conveyance for letters,[6]	81
A knife, spoon, or fork conveyance,	82
A rasping mill,	83

---

1 " For whole cannon."

2 *a whole side of*—wanting.

3 *or ribbon*—wanting.

4 " A continual watch."

5 *A total*—wanting.

6 " 81. 82. Conveyance for letters."

No.

An arithmetical instrument, - - - - - - 84

An untoothsome pear, - - - - - - 85

An imprisoning chair, - - - - - - - 86

A candle mould, - - s - - - - 87

A brazen head, or speaking figure,[1] - - - - 88

Primero gloves,[2] - - - - - - - 89

A dicing-box,[3] - - - - - - - - 90

An artificial ring-horse, - - - - - - 91

A gravel engine, - - - - - - - - 92

A ship-raising engine, - - - - - - 93

A pocket engine to open any door, - - - - 94

A double cross-bow, - - - - - - 95

A way for seabanks, - - - - - - - 96

A perspective instrument, - - - - - - 97

A semi-omnipotent engine, - - - - - - 98

A most admirable way to raise weights,[4] - - - 99

A stupendous water-work, - - - - - 100

---

[1] Wanting entirely in the MS.

[2] "Stamping engine."

[3] "Primero gloves." The Marquis seems to have been in doubt which he should erase—the brazen head or the dicing-box.

[4] Wanting in the MS.

NEW BOOKS AND NEW EDITIONS

PUBLISHED AND FOR SALE BY

THE INDUSTRIAL PUBLICATION CO.,

New York.

Any of these books will be sent to any part of the world on receipt of price. Canadian bills and fractional currency received at par. British postage stamps received at the rate of two cents for one penny. U. S. postage stamps received for fractional parts of a dollar.

New editions of our large catalogue are issued from time to time, and will be sent free to any address. ☞ LIBERAL TERMS TO AGENTS.

Trade "Secrets" and Private Recipes.

A Collection of Recipes, Processes and Formulæ that have been offered for sale at prices varying from 25 cents to $500. With Notes, Corrections, Additions and Special Hints for Improvements. Edited by JOHN PHIN, assisted by an experienced and skilful Pharmacist. Cloth, Gilt Title, - - 60c.

This work was prepared by the author for the purpose of collecting and presenting in a compact form all those recipes and so-called "trade secrets" which have been so extensively advertised and offered for sale. It is not by any means a clap-trap book, though it exposes many clap-traps. It contains a large amount of valuable information that cannot be readily found elsewhere, and it gives not only the formulæ, etc., for manufacturing an immense variety of articles, but important and trustworthy hints as to the best way of making money out of them. Even as a book of recipes it is worth more than its price to any one who is interested in the subjects on which it treats.

The Workshop Companion. Part II. (*Nearly Ready.*)

A Collection of Useful and Reliable Recipes, Rules, Processes, Methods, Wrinkles and Practical Hints. For the Household and the Shop. Neatly bound. Paper, 35c. Cloth, - - - - - - - - - - 60c.

The extraordinary number which has been sold of the First Part of the "Workshop Companion," proves conclusively that such a little work was needed. Having received frequent inquiries for information upon subjects which were not discussed in the First Part, we have had a Second Part prepared for the purpose of supplying the information thus called for. The Second Part has been edited with the same care and thoroughness which did so much towards rendering Part I. a favorite with every worker. The best sources of knowledge have been consulted, and the more important articles have been confided to the hands of specialists of well-known ability.

The two parts will also be issued in one volume, printed on extra paper, and handsomely bound in cloth, with gilt stamp, under the title of THE PRACTICAL ASSISTANT. Price, - - - - - - - - - - - - $1.00

PRACTICAL BOOKS FOR PRACTICAL MEN.

The Steel Square and Its Uses. By Hodgson.

Second and Enlarged Edition, - - - - - - - - $1.00

' This is the only complete work on The Steel Square and Its Uses ever published. It is thorough, exhaustive, clear and easily understood. Confounding terms and scientific phrases have been religiously avoided where possible, and everything in the book has been made so plain that a boy twelve years of age, possessing ordinary intelligence, can understand it from end to end.

The new edition is illustrated with over seventy-five wood cuts, showing how the Square may be used for solving almost every problem in the whole Art of Carpentry.

Stair-Building Made Easy.

Being a Full and Clear Description of the Art of Building the Bodies, Carriages and Cases for all kinds of Stairs and Steps. Together with Illustrations showing the Manner of Laying Out Stairs, Forming Treads and Risers, Building Cylinders, Preparing Strings, with Instructions for Making Carriages for Common, Platform, Dog-Legged, and Winding Stairs. To which is added an Illustrated Glossary of Terms used in Stair-Building, and Designs for Newels, Balusters, Brackets Stair-Mouldings, and Sections of Hand-Rails. By FRED. T. HODGSON. Cloth, Gilt, - - - - - - $1.00

This work takes hold at the very beginning of the subject, and carries the student along by easy stages, until the entire subject of Stair-Building has been unfolded, so far as ordinary practice can ever require. This book and the one on HAND-RAILING, described below, cover nearly the whole subject of STAIR-BUILDING.

A New System of Hand-Railing.

Or, How to Cut Hand-Railing for Circular and other Stairs, Square from the Plank, without the aid of a Falling Mould. The System is New, Novel, Economic, and Easily Learned. Rules, Instructions, and Working Drawing for Building Rails for Seven Different Kinds of Stairs are given. By AN OLD STAIR-BUILDER. Edited and Corrected by FRED. T. HODGSON. Cloth, Gilt, - - - - - - - - - - - - $1.00

The Workshop Companion.

A Collection of Useful and Reliable Recipes. Rules, Processes, Methods, Wrinkles and Practical Hints for the Household and the Shop. Neatly Bound, - - - - - - - - - - - - - 35c.

This is a book of 164 closely printed pages, forming a Dictionary of Practical Information, for Mechanics, Amateurs, Housekeepers, Farmers, Everybody. It is not a mere collection of newspaper clippings, but a series of original treatises on various subjects, such as Alloys, Cements, Inks, Steel, Signal Lights, Polishing Materials, and the art of Polishing Wood, Metals, etc.; Varnishes, Gilding, Silvering, Bronzing, Lacquering, and the working of Brass, Ivory, Alabaster, Iron, Steel, Glass, etc.

Drawing Instruments.

Being a Treatise on Draughting Instruments, with Rules for their Use and Care. Explanations of Scale, Sectors and Protractors. Together with Memoranda for Draughtsmen, Hints on Purchasing Paper, Ink, Instruments, Pencils, etc. Also a Price List of all materials required by Draughtsmen. Illustrated with Twenty-four Explanatory Illustrations. By FRED. T. HODGSON. Paper, - - - - - - - - - - - - 25c.

Practical Carpentry.

Illustrated by Over 300 Engravings. Being a Guide to the Correct Working and Laying Out of all kinds of Carpenters' and Joiners' Work. With the solutions of the various problems in Hip-Roofs, Gothic Work, Centering, Splayed Work, Joints and Jointing, Hinging, Dovetailing, Mitering, Timber Splicing, Hopper Work, Skylights, Raking Mouldings, Circular Work, etc., etc., to which is prefixed a thorough treatise on "Carpenter's Geometry." By FRED. T. HODGSON, author of "The Steel Square and Its Uses," "The Builder's Guide and Estimator's Price Book," "The Slide Rule and How to Use It," etc., etc. Cloth, Gilt, - - - - - - - $1.00

This is the most complete book of the kind ever published. It is thorough, practical and reliable, and at the same time is written in a style so plain that any workman or apprentice can easily understand it.

Hand Saws.

Their Use, Care and Abuse. How to Select and How to File Them. By FRED. T. HODGSON, author of "The Steel Square and Its Uses," "The Builder's Guide and Estimator's Price Book," "Practical Carpentry," etc., etc. Illustrated by Over 75 Engravings. Being a Complete Guide for Selecting, Using and Filing all kinds of Hand Saws, Back Saws, Compass and Key-hole Saws, Web, Hack and Butcher's Saws; showing the Shapes, Forms, Angles, Pitches and Sizes of Saw Teeth suitable for all kinds of Saws, and for all kinds of Wood, Bone, Ivory and Metal ; together with Hints and Suggestions on the choice of Files, Saw Sets, Filing Clamps, and other matters pertaining to the care and management of all classes of hand and other small saws. Cloth, Gilt, - - - - - - - $1.00

The work is intended more particularly for operative Carpenters, Joiners, Cabinet Makers, Carriage Builders and Wood Workers generally, amateurs or professionals.

Plaster : How to Make, and How to Use.

Illustrated with numerous engravings in the text, and Three Plates, giving some Forty Figures of Ceilings, Centrepieces, Cornices, Panels, and Soffits. Being a complete guide for the plasterer, in the preparation and application of all kinds of Plaster, Stucco, Portland Cements, Hydraulic Cements, Lime of Tiel, Rosendale and other Cements. To which is added an Illustrated Glossary of Technical Terms used by plasterers, with hints and suggestions regarding the working, mixing and preparation of scagliola and colored mortars of various kinds. Cloth, Gilt, - - - - - $1.00

Just the book for Plasterers, Bricklayers, Masons, Builders, Architects and Engineers.

The Builder's Guide and Estimator's Price Book.

Being a Compilation of Current Prices of Lumber, Hardware, Glass, Plumbers' Supplies, Paints, Slates, Stones, Limes, Cements, Bricks, Tin, and other Building Materials ; also, Prices of Labor, and Cost of Performing the Several Kinds of Work Required in Building. Together with Prices of Doors, Frames, Sashes, Stairs, Mouldings, Newels, and other Machine Work. To which is appended a large number of Building Rules, Data, Tables, and Useful Memoranda, with a Glossary of Architectural and Building Terms. By FRED. T. HODGSON, Editor of "The Builder and Wood-Worker," Author of "The Steel Square and Its Uses," etc., etc. 12mo., Cloth, - $2.00

Easy Lessons; or, The Stepping Stone to Architecture.

Consisting of a Series of Questions and Answers Explaining in Simple Language the Principles and Progress of Architecture from the earliest times. By THOMAS MITCHELL. Illustrated by nearly 150 Engravings. New Edition with American additions, - - - - - - - 50c.

Architecture is not only a Profession and an Art, but an important branch of every liberal education. No person can be said to be well educated who has not some knowledge of its general principles and of the characteristics of the different styles. The present work is probably the best architectural text-book for beginners ever published. The numerous illustrative engravings make the subject very simple and prevent all misunderstanding. It tells about the different styles, their peculiar features, their origin and the principles that underlie their construction.

Buck's Cottage and Other Designs.

Just the book you want if you are going to build a cheap and comfortable home. It shows a great variety of cheap and medium-priced cottages, besides a number of useful hints and suggestions on the various questions liable to arise in building, such as selection of site, general arrangement or the plans, sanitary questions, etc. Cottages costing from $500 to $5,000 are shown in considerable variety, and nearly every taste can be satisfied. Forty designs for fifty cents. Paper, - - - - - - - 50c.

The information on site, general arrangement of plan, sanitary matters, etc., etc., is worth a great deal more than the cost of the book.

Water-Closets.

A Historical, Mechanical and Sanitary Treatise. By GLENN BROWN, Architect; Associate American Institute of Architects. Neatly Bound in Cloth, with Gilt Title, - - - - - - - - - - - - $1.00

This book contains over 250 Engravings, drawn expressly for the work by the author. The drawings are so clear that the distinctive features of every device are easily seen at a glance, and the descriptions are particularly full and thorough. The paramount importance of this department of the construction of our houses renders all comment upon the value of such a work unnecessary.

Hints and Aids to Builders.

Hints and Aids in Building and Estimating. Gives Hints, Prices, tells how to Measure, explains Building Terms, and, in short, contains a fund of information for all who are interested in building. Paper, - - - 25c.

Common Sense in the Poultry Yard.

A Story of Failures and Successes. Including a full account of 1,000 Hens and What They Did. With a complete description of the Houses, Coops, Fences, Runs, Methods of Feeding, Breeding, Marketing, etc., etc. And Many New Wrinkles and Economical Dodges. By J. P. HAIG. With numerous illustrations. 12mo., Cloth, Gilt, - - - - - $1.00

Hints for Cabinet Makers, Upholsterers, and Furniture Men.

Hints and Practical Information for Cabinet-Makers, Upholsterers, and Fur niture Men generally. Together with a description of all kinds of Finishin; with full directions therefor, Varnishes, Polishes, Stains for Wood, Dyes fo Wood, Gilding and Silvering, Receipts for the Factory, Lacquers, Metal Marbles, etc.; Pictures, Engravings, etc.; Miscellaneous. This work co: tains an immense amount of the most useful information for those who a: engaged in Manufacture, Superintendence, or Construction of Furniture Wood Work of any kind. It is one of the Cheapest and Best Books ev published, and contains over 1,000 Hints, Suggestions, Methods, and D scriptions of Tools, Appliances and Materials. All the Recipes, Rules, a: Directions have been carefully Revised and Corrected by Practical Men great experience, so that they will be found thoroughly trustworthy. Clotl Gilt, - - - - - - - - - - - - - .- - - $1.(

Mechanical Draughting.

The Student's Illustrated Guide to Practical Draughting. A series of Pra tical Instructions for Machinists, Mechanics, Apprentices, and Students Engineering Establishments and Technical Institutes. By T. P. Pemberto: Draughtsman and Mechanical Engineer. Illustrated with numerous e: gravings. Cloth, Gilt, - - - - - - - - - $1.(

This is a simple but thorough book, by a draughtsman of twenty-five year experience. It is intended for beginners and self-taught students, as well as t those who pursue the study under the direction of a teacher.

Lectures in a Workshop.

By T. P. Pemberton, formerly Associate Editor of the "Technologist; Author of "The Student's Illustrated Guide to Practical Draughting." Wit an appendix containing the famous papers by Whitworth "On Plane M tallic Surfaces or True Planes;" "On an Uniform System of Screw Threads; "Address to the Institution of Mechanical Engineers, Glasgow;" "O Standard Decimal Measures of Length." Cloth, Gilt, - - - $1.C

We have here a sprightly, fascinating book, full of valuable hints, interestin anecdotes and sharp sayings. It is not a compilation of dull sermons or dr mathematics, but a live, readable book. The papers by Whitworth, now fir made accessible to the American reader, form the basis of our modern system of accurate work. .

How to Use The Microscope.

By John Phin. Fifth Edition. Greatly enlarged, with over eighty Illustra tions in the Text, and six full page Engravings, printed on heavy tin paper. Cloth, Gilt, - - - - - - - - - - - - $1.0

This is not a book describing *what may be seen* by the microscope, but a simpl and practical work, telling how to use the instrument in its application to th arts. It has been prepared for the use of those who, having no knowledge o the use of the microscope, or, indeed, of any scientific apparatus, desire simpl and practical instruction in the best methods of managing the instrument and

The Engineer's Slide Rule and Its Applications.

A Complete Investigation of the Principles upon which the Slide Rule is Constructed, together with the Method of its Application to all the Purposes of the Practical Mechanic. By William Tonkes. - - 25 cents.

Rhymes of Science: Wise and Otherwise.

By O. W. Holmes, Bret Harte, Ingoldsby, Prof. Forbes, Prof. J. W. McQ. Rankine, Hon. R. W. Raymond, and others. With Illustrations. Cloth, Gilt Title, 50 cents.

We advise all our readers into whose souls the sunlight of fun ever enters to purchase this little book. "Making light of *cereous* things" has been said, by a high authority. to be "a *wicked* profession," but the genius which can balance the ponderosity of an ichthyosaur upon the delicate point of a euphonious rhyme, or bear aloft a bulky leptorhyncus on the sparkling foam of a soul-stirring love ditty, is worthy—worthy of a purchaser.—*Philadelphia Medical News.*

Instruction in the Art of Wood Engraving.

A Manual of Instruction in the Art of Wood Engraving; with a Description of the Necessary Tools and Apparatus, and Concise Directions for their Use; Explanation of the Terms Used, and the Methods Employed for Producing the Various Classes of Wood Engravings. By S. E. Fuller. Fully Illustrated with Engravings by the author, separate sheets of engravings for transfer and practice being added. New Edition, Neatly Bound, - - - - - - 50 cents.

What to Do in Case of Accident.

What to Do and How to Do It in Case of Accident. A Book for Everybody. 12 mo., Cloth, Gilt Title, 50 cents.

This is one of the most useful books ever published. It tells exactly what to do in case of accidents, such as Severe Cuts, Sprains, Dislocations, Broken Bones, Burns with Fire, Scalds, Burns with Corrosive Chemicals. Sunstroke, Suffocation by Foul Air, Hanging, Drowning, Frost-Bite, Fainting, Stings, Bites, Starvation, Lightning, Poisons, Accidents from Machinery and from the Falling of Scaffolding, Gunshot Wounds, etc., etc. It ought to be in every house, for young and old are liable to accident, and the directions given in this book might be the means of saving many a valuable life.

A New Book for Bee-Keepers.

A Dictionary of Practical Apiculture, giving the correct meaning of nearly Five Hundred Terms, according to the usage of the best writers. Intended as a Guide to Uniformity of Expression amongst Bee-Keepers. With Numerous Illustrations, Notes, and Practical Hints. By JOHN PHIN, Author of "How to Use the Microscope," etc. Editor of the "Young Scientist." Price, Cloth, Gilt, . - - - - - . - - - - - 50 cts

This work gives not only the correct meaning of five hundred different words specially used in bee-keeping, but an immense amount of valuable information under the different headings. The labor expended upon it has been very great the definitions having been gathered from the mode in which the words are used by our best writers on bee-keeping, and from the Imperial, Richardson's Skeat's, Websters, Worcester's and other English Dictionaries. The technical information relating to matters connected with bee-keeping has been gathered from the Technical Dictionaries of Brande, Muspratt, Ure, Wagner, Watts, and others. Under the heads *Bee. Comb. Glucose. Honey, Race, Species Sugar, Wax* and others, it brings together a large number of important facts and figures which are now scattered through our bee-literature, and through costly scientific works, and are not easily found when wanted. Here they can be referred to at once under the proper head.

How to Become a Good Mechanic.

Intended as a Practical Guide to Self-taught Men ; telling What to Study What Books to Use ; How to Begin ; What Difficulties will be Met ; How to Overcome Them. In a word, how to carry on such a Course of Self-instruction as will enable the Young Mechanic to rise from the bench to something higher. Paper, - - - - - - - - - - - - 15 cts

This is not a book of "goody-goody" advice, neither is it an advertisement of any special system, nor does it advocate any hobby. It gives plain, practical advice in regard to acquiring that knowledge which alone can enable a young man engaged in any profession or occupation connected with the industrial arts to attain a position higher than that of a mere workman.

Cements and Glue.

A Practical Treatise on the Preparation and Use of all Kinds of Cements Glue, and Paste. By JOHN PHIN, Editor of the "Young Scientist" and the "American Journal of Microscopy." Stiff Covers, - - - 25 cts

Hints for Painters, Decorators and Paperhangers.

Being a selection of Useful Rules, Data, Memoranda, Methods and Suggestions for House, Ship, and Furniture Painting, Paperhanging, Gilding Color Mixing, and other matters Useful and Instructive to Painters and Decorators. Prepared with Special Reference to the Wants of Amateurs By an OLD HAND. - - - - - - - - - - - 25 cts

Any of these books will be sent post paid to any address receipt of price.

The Workshop Companion.

A Collection of Useful and Reliable Recipes, Rules, Processes, Methods, Wrinkles and Practical Hints for the Household and the Shop. Neatly Bound - - - - - - - - - - - - - - 35c.

This is a book of 164 closely printed pages, forming a Dictionary of Practical Information, for Mechanics, Amateurs, Housekeepers, Farmers, Everybody. It is not a mere collection of newspaper clippings, but a series of original treatises on various subjects. such as Alloys, Cements, Inks, Steel, Signal Lights, Polishing Materials, and the art of Polishing Wood, Metals, etc.; Varnishes, Gilding, Silvering, Bronzing, Lacquering, and the working of Brass, Ivory, Alabaster, Iron, Steel, Glass, etc.

Carpenter's and Joiner's Pocket Companion.

Containing Rules, Data and Directions for Laying Out Work and for Calculating and Estimating. Compiled by THOMAS MOLONEY, Carpenter and Joiner. Neatly Bound in Cloth, with Gilt Stamp and Red Edges. - 50 cts.

This is a compact and handy little volume, containing enough matter that is not easily found anywhere else to make it worth more than its price to every intelligent carpenter.

Hints for Painters, Decorators and Paperhangers.

Being a selection of Useful Rules, Data, Memoranda, Methods and Suggestions for House, Ship, and Furniture Painting, Paperhanging, Gilding, Color Mixing, and other matters Useful and Instructive to Painters and Decorators. Prepared with Special Reference to the Wants of Amateurs. By an OLD HAND, - - - - - - - - - - - - - - - 25 cts.

Drawing Instruments.

Being a Treatise on Draughting Instruments, with Rules for their Use and Care, Explanations of Scale, Sectors and Protractors. Together with Memooranda for Draughtsmen, Hints on Purchasing Paper, Ink, Instruments, Pencils, etc. Also a Price List of all materials required by Draughtsmen. Illustrated with Twenty-four Explanatory Illustrations. By FRED. T. HODGSON. Paper, - - - - - - - - - - - - - - 25c.

Cements and Glue.

A Practical Treatise on the Preparation and Use of all kinds of Cements, Glue and Paste. By JOHN PHIN, author of "How to Use the Microscope." Paper, - - - - - - - - - - - - - - - 25 cts.

Contains nearly 200 recipes for the preparation of Cements for almost every conceivable purpose.

Common Sense in the Poultry Yard - - - - -	$ .00
What to Do in Case of Accident - - - - -	50c.
How to Become a Good Mechanic - - - - -	15c
Rhymes of Science: Wise and Otherwise - - - -	50c.
Shooting on the Wing - - - - - -	75c.
The Pistol, and How to Use It - - - - -	50c.

Any of these books will be sent post paid to any address on receipt of price.

Shooting on the Wing.

Plain Directions for Acquiring the Art of Shooting on the Wing. With Useful Hints concerning all that relates to Guns and Shooting, and particularly in regard to the art of Loading so as to Kill. To which has been added several Valuable and hitherto Secret Recipes, of Great Practical Importance to the Sportsman. By an Old Gamekeeper.

12mo., Cloth, Gilt Title.　　-　　-　　-　　75 cents

The Pistol as a Weapon of Defence,

In the House and on the Road.

12mo., Cloth. -　　-　　-　　-　　-　　50 cents

This work aims to instruct the peaceable and law-abiding citizen in the best means of protecting themselves from the attacks of the brutal and the lawless, and is the only practical book published on this subject. Its contents are as follows: The Pistol as a Weapon of Defence.—The Carrying of Fire-Arms.—Different kinds of Pistols in Market; How to Choose a Pistol.—Ammunition, different kinds Powder, Caps, Bullets, Copper Cartridges, etc.—Best form of Bullet.— How to Load.—Best Charge for Pistols.—How to regulate the Charge.—Care of the Pistol; how to Clean it.—How to Handle and Carry the Pistol.—How to Learn to Shoot.—Practical use of the Pistol; how to Protect yourself and how to Disable your antagonist.

Lightning Rods.

Plain Directions for the Construction and Erection of Lightning Rods. By John Phin, C. E., editor of "The Young Scientist," author of "Chemical History of the Six Days of the Creation," etc. Second Edition. Enlarged and Fully Illustrated.

12mo., Cloth, Gilt Title.　　-　　-　　-　　50 cents

This is a simple and practical little work, intended to convey just such information as will enable every property owner to decide whether or not his buildings are thoroughly protected. It is not written in the interest of any patent or particular article of manufacture, and by following its directions, any ordinarily skilful mechanic can put up a rod that will afford perfect protection, and that will not infringe any patent. Every owner of a house or barn ought to procure a copy.

Hours with a Three-Inch Telescope.

By Capt. WILLIAM NOBLE, F. R. A. S., F. R. M. S., Honorary Associate of the Liverpool Astronomical Society, etc. 12mo., Cloth, - - $1.50

This book is even more elementary and practical than Webb's "Celestial Objects. It has been written to furnish the very beginner in observational astronomy with such directions as shall enable him to employ, to the greatest possible advantage, the kind of instrument with which he will, in all probability, at first provide himself.

Like our edition of Webb, the book has been made for us by the English publishers, and is in all respects the same as the English edition.

Celestial Objects for Common Telescopes.

By the Rev. T. W. WEBB, M. A., F. R. A. S. Fourth Edition, Revised and Greatly Enlarged. Fully Illustrated with Engravings and a large Map of the Moon. Cloth, - - - - - - - - - , - - $3.00

This edition has been made for us by the English publishers, and is in every respect the same as the English edition. The work itself is too well known to require commendation at our hands. No one that owns even the commonest kind of a telescope can afford to do without it.

"Many things deemed invisible to secondary instruments, are plain enough to one who knows how to see them."—SMYTH.

"When an object is once discerned by a superior power, an inferior one will suffice to see it afterwards."—SIR W. HERSCHELL.

The Sun.

A Familiar Description of His Phenomena. By the Rev. THOMAS WILLIAM WEBB, M. A., F. R. A. S., author of "Celestial Objects for Common Telescopes." With Numerous Illustrations. Cloth, - - - - 40c.

This work gives in a delightfully popular style an account of the most recent discoveries in regard to the Sun. It is very freely illustrated.

Chemical History of the Six Days of Creation.

By JOHN PHIN, author of "How to Use the Microscope." 12mo., Cloth 75c.

In this volume an attempt is made to trace the evolution of our globe from the primeval state of nebulous mist, "without form and void," and existing in "darkness." or with an entire absence of the manifestations of the physical forces, to the condition in which it was fitted to become the habitation of man. While the statements and conclusions are rigidly scientific, it gives some exceedingly novel views of a rather hackneyed subject.

Microscope Objectives.

The Angular Aperture of Microscope Objectives. By Dr. GEORGE E. BLACKHAM. 8vo., Cloth. Eighteen full page Illustrations printed on extra fine paper, - - - - - - - - - - - - - - $1.25

This is the elaborate paper on Angular Aperture, read by Dr. Blackham before the Microscopical Congress, held at Indianapolis.

Marvels of Pond Life.

A Year's Microscopic Recreations Among the Polyps. Infusoria, Rotifers, Water Bears and Polyzoa. By HENRY J. SLACK, F. G. S., F. R. M. S., etc. Second Edition. Seven full page Plates and Numerous Wood Engravings in the text. 12mo., Cloth, - - - - - - - - - $1.00

Section Cutting.

A Practical Guide to the Preparation and Mounting of Sections for the Microscope; Special Prominence being given to the Subject of Animal Sections By Sylvester Marsh. Reprinted from the London edition. With Illustrations. 12mo., Cloth, Gilt Title.   · 75 cents.

This is undoubtedly the most thorough treatise extant upon section cutting in all its details. The American edition has been greatly enlarged by valuable explanatory notes, and also by extended directions, illustrated with engravings, for selecting and sharpening knives and razors.

A Book for Beginners with the Microscope.

Being an abridgment of "Practical Hints on the Selection and Use of the Microscope." By John Phin. Fully illustrated, and neatly and strongly bound in boards. 30 cts.

This book was prepared for the use of those who, having no knowledge of the use of the microscope, or, indeed, of any scientific apparatus, desire simple and practical instruction in the best methods of managing the instrument and preparing objects.

How to Use the Microscope.

"Practical Hints on the Selection and Use of the Microscrope." Intended for Beginners. By John Phin, Editor of the "American Journal of Microscopy." Fourth Edition. Greatly enlarged, with over 80 engravings in the text, and 6 full-page engravings, printed on heavy tint paper. 12mo., cloth, gilt title,   - $1.00

The Microscope.

By Andrew Ross. Fully Illustrated. 12mo., Cloth, Gilt Title.   -   -   -   -   -   75 cents.

This is the celebrated article contributed by Andrew Ross to the "Penny Cyclopædia," and quoted so frequently by writers on the Microscope Carpenter and Hogg, in the last editions of their works on the Microscope, and Brooke, in his treatise on Natural Philosophy, all refer to this article as the best source for full and clear information in regard to the principles upon which the modern achromatic Microscope is constructed. It should be in the library of every person to whom the Microscope is more than a toy. It is written in simple language, free from abstruse technicalities.

FOURTH EDITION. Greatly Enlarged, with over 80 illustrations in the Text and 6 full page Engravings, printed on Heavy Tint Paper. 1 Vol. 12mo., 240 pages. Neatly Bound in Cloth, Gilt Title. Price $1.00.

HOW TO USE THE MICROSCOPE.

A SIMPLE AND PRACTICAL BOOK, INTENDED FOR BEGINNERS.

By JOHN PHIN,

Editor of " The American Journal of Microscopy."

CONDENSED TABLE OF CONTENTS.

THE MICROSCOPE.—What it Is; What it Does; Different Kinds of Microscopes; Principles of its Construction; Names of the Different Parts.

SIMPLE MICROSCOPES.—Hand Magnifiers; Doublets; Power of Two or More Lenses When Used Together; Stanhope Lens; Coddington Lens; Achromatic Doublets and Triplets; Twenty-five Cent Microscopes—and How to Make Them; Penny Microscopes, to Show Eels in Paste and Vinegar.

DISSECTING MICROSCOPES.—Essentials of a Good Dissecting Microscope.

COMPOUND MICROSCOPES.—Cheap Foreign Stands; The Ross Model; The Jackson Model; The Continental Model; The New American Model; Cheap American Stands; The Binocular Microscope; The Binocular Eye-piece; The Inverted Microscope; Lithological Microscopes; The Aquarium Microscope; Microscopes for Special Purposes; "Class" Microscopes.

OBJECTIVES.—Defects of Common Lenses; Spherical Aberration; Chromatic do.; Corrected Objectives; Defining Power; Achromatism; Aberration; Form; Flatness of Field; Angular Aperture; Penetrating Power; Working Distance; Immersion and "Homogeneous" Lenses; Duplex Fronts; French Triplets, etc., etc.

TESTING OBJECTIVES.—General Rules; Accepted Standards—Diatoms, Ruled Lines, Artificial Star; Podura; Nobert's Lines; Möller's Probe Platte, etc., etc.

SELECTION OF A MICROSCOPE.—Must be Adapted to Requirements and Skill of User; Microscopes for Botany; For Physicians; For Students.

ACCESSORY APPARATUS.—Stage Forceps; Forceps Carrier; Plain Slides; Concave Slides; Watch-Glass Holder; Animalcule Cage; Zoophyte Trough; The Weber Slide; The Cell-Trough; The Compressorium; Gravity Compressorium; Growing Slides; Frog Plate; Table; Double Nose-piece.

ILLUMINATION.—Sun-Light; Artificial Light—Candles, Gas, Lamps, etc., etc.

ILLUMINATION OF OPAQUE OBJECTS.—Bulls-Eye Condenser; Side Reflector; The Lieberkuhn; The Parabolic Reflector; Vertical Illuminators.

ILLUMINATION OF TRANSPARENT OBJECTS.—Direct and Reflected Light; Axial or Central Light; Oblique Light; The Achromatic Condenser; The Webster Condenser, and How to Use it; Wenham's Reflex Illuminator, and How to Use it; The Wenham Prism; The "Half-Button;" The Woodward Illuminator; Tolles' Illuminating Traverse Lens; The Spot Lens; The Parabolic Illuminator; Polarized Light.

HOW TO USE THE MICROSCOPE.—General Rules; Hints to Beginners.

HOW TO USE OBJECTIVES OF LARGE APERTURE.—Collar-Correction, etc.

CARE OF THE MICROSCOPE.—Should be Kept Covered; Care of Objectives; Precautions to be Used when Corrosive Vapors and Liquids are Employed; To Protect th Objectives from Vapors which Corrode Glass; Cleaning the Objectives; Cleaning th Brass Work.

COLLECTING OBJECTS.—Where to Find Objects; What to Look for; How to Capture Them.

THE PREPARATION AND EXAMINATION OF OBJECTS.—Cutting Thin Sections of Soft Substances; Valentine's Knife; Sections of Wood and Bone; Improved Section Cutter; Sections of Rock; Knives; Scissors; Needles; Dissecting Pans and Dishes; Dissecting Microscopes; Separation of Deposits from Liquids; Preparing Whole Insects; Feet, Eyes, Tongues, Wings, etc , of Insects; Use of Chemical Tests; Liquids for Moistening Objects; Refractive Powers of Different Liquids; Iod-Serum; Artificial Iod-Serum; Covers for Keeping Out Dust; Errors in Microscopic Observations.

PRESERVATIVE PROCESSES.—General Principles; Preservative Media.

APPARATUS FOR MOUNTING OBJECTS.—Slides; Covers; Cells; Turn-Tables, etc.

CEMENTS AND VARNISHES.—General Rules for Using.

MOUNTING OBJECTS.—Mounting Transparent Objects Dry; in Balsam; in Liquids; Whole Insects; How to Get Rid of Air-Bubbles; Mounting Opaque Objects.

FINISHING THE SLIDES.—Cabinets; Maltwood Finder; Microscopical Fallacies.

A NEW SERIES OF PRACTICAL BOOKS.

WORK MANUALS.

The intention of the publishers is to give in this Series a number of small books which will give Thorough and Reliable Information in the plainest possible language, upon the

ARTS OF EVERYDAY LIFE.

Each volume will be by some one who is not only practically familiar with his subject, but who has the ability to make it clear to others. The volumes will each contain from 50 to 75 pages, will be neatly and clearly printed on good paper and bound in tough and durable binding. The price will be *25 cents each, or five for One Dollar.*
The following are the titles of the volumes already issued. Others will follow at short intervals.

I. Cements and Glue.

A Practical Treatise on the Preparation and Use of All Kinds of Cements, Glue and Paste. By JOHN PHIN, Editor of the *Young Scientist* and the *American Journal of Microscopy*
Every mechanic and householder will find this volume of almost everyday use. It contains nearly 200 recipes for the preparation of Cements for almost every conceivable purpose.

II. The Slide Rule, and How to Use It.

This is a compilation of Explanations, Rules and Instructions suitable for mechanics and others interested in the industrial arts. Rules are given for the measurement of all kinds of boards and planks, timber in the round or square, glaziers' work and painting, brickwork, paviors' work, tiling and slating, the measurement of vessels of various shapes, the wedge, inclined planes, wheels and axles, levers, the weighing and measurement of metals and all solid bodies, cylinders, cones, globes, octagon rules and formulæ, the measurement of circles, and a comparison of French and English measures, with much other information, useful to builders, carpenters, bricklayers, glaziers, paviors, slaters, machinists and other mechanics.
Possessed of this little Book and a good Slide Rule, mechanics might carry in their pockets some hundreds of times the power of calculation that they now have in their heads, and the use of the instrument is very easily acquired.

III. Hints for Painters, Decorators and Paperhangers.

Being a selection of Useful Rules, Data, Memoranda, Methods and Suggestions for House, Ship, and Furniture Painting, Paperhanging, Gilding, Color Mixing, and other matters Useful and Instructive to Painters and Decorators. Prepared with Special Reference to the Wants of Amateurs. By an Old Hand.

IV. Construction, Use and Care of Drawing Instruments.

Being a Treatise on Draughting Instruments, with Rules for their Use and Care, Explanations of Scale, Sectors and Protractors. Together with Memoranda for Draughtsmen, Hints on Purchasing Paper, Ink, Instruments, Pencils, etc. Also a Price List of all materials required by Draughtsmen. Illustrated with twenty-four Explanatory Illustrations. By FRED. T. HODGSON.

V. The Steel Square.

Some Difficult Problems in Carpentry and Joinery Simplified and Solved by the aid of the Carpenters' Steel Square, together with a Full Description of the Tool, and Explanations of the Scales, Lines and Figures on the Blade and Tongue, and How to Use them in Everyday Work. Showing how the Square may be Used in Obtaining the Lengths and Bevels of Rafters, Hips, Groins, Braces, Brackets, Purlins, Collar-Beams, and Jack-Rafters. Also, its Application in Obtaining the Bevels and Cuts for Hoppers, Spring Mouldings, Octagons, Diminished Styles, etc., etc. Illustrated by Numerous Wood-cuts. By FRED. T. HODGSON, Author of the "Carpenters' Steel Square."

Note.—This work is intended as an elementary introduction for the use of those who have not time to study Mr. Hodgson's larger work on the same subject.

THE WORKSHOP COMPANION.

A Collection of Useful and Reliable Recipes, Rules, Processes, Methods, Wrinkles, and Practical Hints,

FOR THE HOUSEHOLD AND THE SHOP.

CONTENTS.

Abyssinian Gold;—Accidents, General Rules;—Alabaster, how to work, polish and clean;—Alcohol;—Alloys, rules for making, and 26 recipes;—Amber, how to work, polish and mend;—Annealing and Hardening glass, copper, steel, etc.;—Arsenical Soap;—Arsenical Powder;—Beeswax, how to bleach;—Blackboards, how to make;—Brass, how to work, polish, color, varnish, whiten, deposit by electricity, clean, etc., etc.;—Brazing and Soldering;—Bronzing brass, wood, leather, etc.;—Burns, how to cure;—Case-hardening;—Catgut, how prepared;—Cements, general rules for using, and 56 recipes for preparing;—Copper, working, welding, depositing;—Coral, artificial;—Cork, working;—Crayons for Blackboards;—Curling brass, iron, etc.;—Liquid Cuticle;—Etching copper, steel, glass;—Eye, accidents to;—Fires, to prevent;—Clothes on Fire;—Fireproof Dresses;—Fly Papers;—Freezing Mixtures, 6 recipes;—Fumigating Pastils;—Gilding metal, leather, wood, etc.;—Glass, cutting, drilling, turning in the lathe, fitting stoppers, removing tight stoppers, powdering, packing, imitating ground glass, washing glass vessels, etc.;—Grass, Dry, to stain;—Guns, to make shoot close, to keep from rusting, to brown the barrels of, etc., etc.;—Handles, to fasten;—Inks, rules for selecting and preserving, and 34 recipes for;—Ink Eraser;—Inlaying;—Iron, forging, welding, case-hardening, zincing, tinning, do. in the cold, brightening, etc., etc.;—Ivory, to work, polish, bleach, etc.;—Javelle Water;—Jewelry and Gilded Ware, care of, cleaning, coloring, etc.;—Lacquer, how to make and apply;—Laundry Gloss;—Skeleton Leaves;—Lights, signal and colored, also for tableaux, photography, etc., 25 · recipes;—Lubricators, selection of, 4 recipes for;—Marble, working, polishing, cleaning;—Metals, polishing;—Mirrors, care of, to make, pure silver, etc., etc.;—Nickel, to plate with without a battery;—Noise, prevention of;—Painting Bright Metals;—Paper, adhesive, barometer, glass, tracing, transfer, waxed, etc.;—Paper, to clean, take creases out of, remove water stains, mount drawing paper, to prepare for varnishing, etc., etc.;—Patina;—Patterns, to trace;—Pencils, indelible;—Pencil Marks, to fix;—Pewter;—Pillows for Sick Room, cheap and good;—Plaster-of-Paris, how to work;—Poisons, antidotes for, 12 recipes;—Polishing Powders, preparation and use of (six pages);—Resins, their properties, etc.;—Saws, how to sharpen;—Sieves;—Shellac, properties and uses of;—Silver, properties of, oxidized, old, cleaning, to remove ink stains from, to dissolve from plated goods, etc., etc.;—Silvering metals, leather, iron, etc.;—Size, preparation of various kinds of;—Skins, tanning and curing, do with hair on;—Stains, to remove from all kinds of goods;—Steel, tempering and working (six pages);—Tin, properties, methods of working;—Varnish, 21 recipes for;—Varnishing, directions for;—Voltaic Batteries;—Watch, care of;—Waterproofing, 7 recipes for;—Whitewash;—Wood Floors, waxing, staining, and polishing;—Wood, polishing;—Wood, staining, 17 recipes;—Zinc, to pulverize, black varnish for.

164 closely-printed pages, neatly bound.   Sent by mail for 36 cents (postage stamps received).

NEW DESIGNS

FOR

Fret or Scroll Sawyers.

MR. F. T. HODGSON, whose admirable series of articles on the USE OF THE SCROLL SAW are now in course of publication in the YOUNG SCIENTIST, has prepared for us a series of

SEVENTEEN DESIGNS,

of which the following is a list:

No. 1.—This shows one side, back, and bottom, of a pen rack. It may be made of ebony, walnut, or other dark wood.

No. 2.—Design for inlaying drawer fronts, table tops, box lids, and many other things. It is a sumach leaf pattern.

No. 3.—Design for a thermometer stand. It may be made of any hard wood or alabaster. The method of putting together is obvious.

No. 4.—This shows a design for a lamp screen. The open part may be covered with tinted silk, or other suitable material, with some appropriate device worked on with the needle, or, if preferred, ornaments may be painted on the silk, etc.

No. 5.—A case for containing visiting cards. Will look best made of white holly.

No. 6.—A placque stand. it may be made of any kind of dark or medium wood.

No. 7.—A design for ornaments suitable for a window cornice. It should be made of black walnut, and overlaid on some light colored hard wood.

No. 8—A design for a jewel casket. This will be very pretty made of white holly and lined with blue velvet It also looks well made of ebony lined with crimson.

No. 9.—Frame. Will look well made of any dark wood.

No. 10.—Frame. Intended to be made in pairs. Looks well made of white holly, with leaves and flowers painted on wide stile.

No. 11.—Horseshoe. Can be made of any kind of wood and used for a pen rack. When decorated with gold and colors, looks very handsome.

No. 12.—Design for a hinge strap. If made of black walnut, and planted on a white or oaken door, will look well.

No. 13.—Design for a napkin ring. May be made of any kind of hard wood.

No. 14.—Hinge strap for doors with narrow stiles.

No. 15.—Centre ornament for panel.

No. 16.—Corner ornament for panel.

No. 17.—Key-hole escutcheon.

These designs we have had photo-lithographed and printed on good paper, so that the outlines are sharp, and the opposite sides of each design symmetrical. Common designs are printed from coarse wooden blocks, and are rough and unequal, so that it is often impossible to make good work from them.

The series embraces over forty different pieces, and designs of equal quality cannot be had for less than five, ten or fifteen cents each. We offer them for twenty-five cents for the set, which is an average price of only one cent and a half each.

Mailed to any address on receipt of price.

SHEET NO. 1.

SHEET NO. 2.

REDUCED FIGURES OF
NEW DESIGNS FOR FRET OR SCROLL SAWYERS.
SIZE OF SHEETS 28 BY 22 INCHES.
(For description see preeeding page.)